A Startling Confession

"The boy doesn't understand, Constable Snow," Dr. Gladstone said.

He turned back to Lucas. "Listen to me carefully, Lucas. I want you to tell me how you got the org—the heart in the first place."

Lucas stared at him, uncomprehending.

"Where did you get the heart?" Snow said again, enunciating each word.

"Out of here," Lucas said, pointing to his chest.

"Out of your own chest?"

Lucas laughed and looked down at his intact chest.

"Lucas!" Snow spoke sharply to get the boy's attention and to distract him from his laughter. It worked. The boy's eyes locked onto his own. "You would have to cut that heart out of a person. Is that how you got it? Did you cut it out?"

Lucas's eyes became unfocused for a moment as if he had moved his soul to another location, but he slowly rejoined himself and brought his attention back to Snow. "Yes," he said, nodding his head. "I think so."

Dr. Alexandra Gladstone Mysteries
by Paula Paul

SYMPTOMS OF DEATH
AN IMPROPER DEATH
HALF A MIND TO MURDER

Half a Mind
to Murder

Paula Paul

BERKLEY PRIME CRIME, NEW YORK

If you purchased this book without a cover, you should be aware that this book is stolen property. It was reported as "unsold and destroyed" to the publisher, and neither the author nor the publisher has received any payment for this "stripped book."

This is a work of fiction. Names, characters, places, and incidents either are the product of the author's imagination or are used fictitiously, and any resemblance to actual persons, living or dead, business establishments, events, or locales is entirely coincidental.

HALF A MIND TO MURDER

A Berkley Prime Crime Book / published by arrangement with the author

PRINTING HISTORY
Berkley Prime Crime mass-market edition / October 2003

Copyright © 2003 by Paula Paul.
Cover art by Bryan Haynes.
Cover design by Judith Murello.
Text design by Julie Rogers.

All rights reserved.
This book, or parts thereof, may not be reproduced in any form without permission.
The scanning, uploading, and distribution of this book via the Internet or via any other means without the permission of the publisher is illegal and punishable by law. Please purchase only authorized electronic editions, and do not participate in or encourage electronic piracy of copyrighted materials. Your support of the author's rights is appreciated.
For information address: The Berkley Publishing Group,
a division of Penguin Group (USA) Inc.,
375 Hudson Street, New York, New York 10014.

ISBN: 0-425-19282-2

Berkley Prime Crime Books are published by
The Berkley Publishing Group,
a division of Penguin Group (USA) Inc.,
375 Hudson Street, New York, New York 10014.
The name BERKLEY PRIME CRIME
and the BERKLEY PRIME CRIME design
are trademarks belonging to Penguin Group (USA) Inc.

PRINTED IN THE UNITED STATES OF AMERICA

10 9 8 7 6 5 4 3 2 1

*For UCI, who helped
"midwife" this story*

1

Men of the town Newton-Upon-Sea were dying at an alarming rate. Harry Neill died first in early June, then his brother, Winslow, succumbed a few weeks later, followed by Frewin Millsap.

It was a mysterious illness that took them. Ben Milligan had contracted the malady shortly after Harry's death, and he was the only one of the four the local surgeon, Dr. Alexandra Gladstone, was able to save.

Harry's illness started with a carbuncle on his forearm. He let it develop to an advanced state before he sought the doctor's help. She treated it with a caustic of potash and applied a poultice made of wild indigo leaves, marsh-mallow, and ground centaury leaves.

The carbuncle, however, grew to six inches in diameter and rapidly proceeded to a state of gangrene. Openings formed in the mass, oozing a bad-smelling, dark bloody liquid, so that Dr. Gladstone was compelled to add yeast and charcoal to the poultice to counter the odor. Meanwhile, other small pimples appeared on his arm that threatened to develop into more carbuncles.

Soon, Harry was prostrate with a raging fever, and Dr. Gladstone suspected infection from the carbuncle had somehow gotten into his bloodstream. He died within a few weeks from the day he first came to her for help.

Shortly after his death, his brother, Winslow, several years younger, developed a series of carbuncles even more serious than Harry's, along with a lung infection, and died within a month, in spite of Alexandra's attempts to help him. She was concerned and puzzled. When a third patient, Ben Milligan, a tenent farmer from the nearby estate of the earl of Dunsford, came to her with symptoms of the same skin disorder, she was alarmed. Ben's condition proved to be self-limiting, however, and he survived. Alexandra had no idea why he recovered while the other two had not, and further, she was troubled that she couldn't pinpoint a cause for the eruptions. She was even more troubled when she learned that Frewin Millsap, a carpenter, had died of similar symptoms but had never sent for her.

According to Dr. Gladstone's medical training, carbuncles that proved difficult to treat or that resulted in death were most likely to appear in middle-aged men given to intemperance and debauchery or who were mentally depressed.

None of the men fit that description except to the extent that they were all middle-aged or, in Ferwin's case, a bit past that mark. Harry was a respectable widower who owned the apothecary in Newton-Upon-Sea, a medium-sized village on the Essex coast where Alexandra maintained her practice. His profession led him initially to self-treatment, which explained his delay in visiting the doctor. His brother, Winslow, ran a shop that sold supplies to support the local oyster fishing industry and led a quiet life with his wife and three nearly grown daughters. Ben, somewhat older than the brothers, took pride in the vegetables he sold each market day. None of the three, it seemed, would have had time for intemperance or debauchery, and none showed signs of mental depression.

Alexandra had discussed the puzzling aspects of the carbuncle cases with Nancy, her nurse, who also served as her maid-of-all-work. Nancy, who had equally as much medical experience as Alexandra if not the education, was also puzzled. Unlike Alexandra, however, she did not dwell overly long on the puzzle. Her current concern was for Polly Cobbe, who had been Harry Neill's sole employee since his rather unpleasant young apprentice left without notice. Polly was a tall, blond woman of about forty, given to plumpness. She possessed a fine intellect that made her an interesting conversationalist. Her function at the apothecary had been to keep the shelves straight and to help Harry with his accounting records. At Harry's death, the shop was closed, and Polly, who, though she possessed at least some education, was unable to find employment except as a charwoman at the local tavern, known as the Blue Ram.

Nancy had brought up the fact more than once that it was her opinion that, given Miss Cobbe's intelligence, she would have been able to find something more suitable had she been a man. It was, she said, "entirely inexcusable that a woman of Miss Cobbe's grace and temperament should be reduced to cleaning up after drunks."

Alexandra knew where this was leading.

"You know, I could use a bit of help around here." Nancy breathed a rather theatrical sigh as she spoke and filled Alexandra's plate with boiled mutton and potatoes.

Alexandra glanced at Nancy from across the kitchen

table, where it was their custom to eat together. "What are you getting at?" she asked. "You've always been quite defensive if I ever suggested hiring someone to help you."

"I'm not as young as I used to be, you know."

"Indeed." Alexandra cut off a tiny morsel of the mutton and made no attempt to keep the cynicism out of her voice. "I suppose you've aged considerably in the month since I last mentioned it." Zack, her black-and-white Newfoundland whose huge body was curled at her feet, raised his head and glanced with what appeared to be a bored look, first at Alexandra and then Nancy.

Nancy kept her eyes down, sawing vigorously with her knife on her own chunk of mutton. "It's just that the patient load is increasing, and my duties as your nurse must take precedent over everything else. I could use a bit of help with the cooking. It could be you would like a change from my plain English fare. Perhaps a little . . . oh, say, French cuisine would do you good."

Alexandra swallowed the bit of potato she had just eaten. There had been no need to chew, since the potato immediately turned to mush as soon as she placed it in her mouth. "French cuisine? Really? Don't you always say the way the French cook isn't good for a person? All those heavy cream sauces and everything dipped in butter?"

Nancy shrugged and was uncharacteristically quiet for a moment. Alexandra had known Nancy since they were both children. Nancy's mother had been the late Dr. Gladstone's maid-of-all-work from the time he had married Alexandra's mother. She'd been an enormous help to him in helping him raise Alexandra after his wife died when Alexandra was ten years old. Having been together all their lives, Nancy and Alexandra had been as close as sisters, in spite of the difference in their class. The late

Dr. Gladstone had been as fond of the precocious Nancy as Alexandra was, although he often gave his daughter halfhearted warnings that she was not cultivating the proper mistress-servant relationship with the willful servant child. However, it was he himself who'd insisted that Nancy sit in with Alexandra while she was being tutored at home, since, being female, neither of them was allowed to attend the local school.

Thanks, in part, to her father's influence, as well as to a change in English law, Alexandra had been one of a few women admitted to university to study medicine while Nancy remained at home to act as the late doctor's nurse, her sharp and eager mind observing and taking in more medical knowledge than many physicians possessed. Then the late Dr. Gladstone had sent her for a brief course held at Bradfordshire Hospital and sponsored by the Florence Nightingale Academy in London. After the doctor's death, Alexandra took over his practice, and Nancy became her nurse.

Alexandra was beginning to wonder about Nancy's long silence. It certainly wasn't like her to be at a loss for words. When it appeared Nancy would remain silent, Alexandra spoke. "Polly Cobbe is as English as we are. What would she know about French cuisine?"

Nancy looked up suddenly from her plate and feigned innocence. "Polly Cobbe? Why would you bring her up?"

"I didn't. You did."

"I beg your pardon, Miss Alex, I never—"

"You want me to hire her to get her out of that tavern."

Nancy smiled broadly and pretended surprise. "What a wonderful idea! And so generous of you."

Alexandra played her game. "Oh, that isn't what you were thinking? Then you won't mind if I tell you I won't hire her."

"You won't hire her?" Nancy's alarm was genuine. "Why not? You just admitted you'd been thinking of hiring someone to help me."

"I was thinking of part time, Nancy. Maybe once a week to help with the baking. You know as well as I the status of my income and expenses. And anyway, we don't really know this woman. It's possible she's a terrible cook."

Nancy pretended to be disinterested. "Oh, I know her well enough, I'd say. 'Twas I you always sent to fetch the ingredients you needed from the apothecary, you know. So I got to know Polly, now didn't I? She's a proper sort, I can tell you that. Spent some time in France as it happens. Working as a maid in the home of some gentleman, was a maid-of-all-work, same as myself, she told me. So we talked recipes, naturally. She even wrote some of them down for me, but it's not my style, now is it? French cuisine. Nevertheless, you know I would never steer you wrong, would I? You didn't go wrong when you hired Rob and Artie as stable boys when I recommended them, did you?"

"As I recall," Alexandra said, laying her napkin aside, "it was you who hired Rob and Artie, and without even asking me."

"Well . . ." The expression on Nancy's face was only slightly apologetic before enthusiasm took over. "It worked out quite well, you'll have to admit."

Alexandra gave her a noncommittal "mmm" as she stood and started toward the door, on her way to open the surgery to receive walk-in patients. Rob and Artie, two homeless young ruffians from the docks whom Nancy had rescued from their previous profession as petty thieves, had indeed become excellent stable boys. But she wasn't going to admit that at the moment and give the wily Nancy an even better advantage.

"So you'll hire her then, at least part time?" Nancy called after her.

"We shall see." She turned back to signal Zack to follow her just in time to see the satisfied smile on Nancy's face. "That doesn't mean yes, Nancy. It simply means I'll think about it."

"Of course, miss." Nancy's knowing smile disappeared, but her expression, in spite of her attempt to cover it, remained annoyingly self-assured.

The first of Alexandra's patients was already waiting outside the door to the surgery when she unlocked it. The surgery's waiting room entrance was located at ground level on the south end of her house, which was shaded by several large oak trees along with a few beech. Lucas Pendennis, a young man of perhaps sixteen years, sat under one of the oak trees, his back resting against the enormous trunk. Lucas, whose mother was a lace dealer, was mentally deficient. Most people referred to him as *the idjet Pendennis*. Alexandra knew the correct medical term for Lucas was *imbecile* rather than idiot, since, although his intelligence was limited, he possessed the ability to speak, to express feelings and emotions, and to carry out certain simple instructions. He was also capable of reasoning to a limited extent. It was not at all unexpected for him to show up at the surgery on rare occasion with a painful cut or bruise, having learned that the doctor was in possession of the means to help him heal or to stop hurting. He was a gentle boy and quite likable in Alexandra's mind, in spite of his sometimes strange habits. He was, for example, fond of wandering the sea coast or the sparsely wooded hills and dales at night, often singing to himself, or even howling like a hound or hooting like an owl. He claimed to be communicating with the animals, and he was particularly fond of creatures of all kinds, both domestic and wild. People claimed to have seen him in the woods surrounded by foxes and badgers, and he'd once captured a wild hare and kept her as a pet until, so he claimed, she told him she wanted to return to the wild.

Most people didn't share Alexandra's fondness for him. He was often taunted and teased by children and adults alike, and many feared him because of his strange ways. Some, because of his Cornish name and ancestry, thought him to be a Celtic witch.

Alexandra opened the door and called to him. Still slumped against the tree, he raised his head to look at her, and she saw to her surprise and dismay that he was crying.

"Lucas! What's wrong?" She stepped outside and walked toward him as he stood up and lumbered toward her, sniffing and wiping at his nose with the back of his hand. He seemed unable to speak. Alexandra led him gently into the surgery and gave him a handkerchief to blow his nose. "Have you hurt yourself, Lucas?"

Lucas shook his head and looked at her, his face contorted with emotion. "Wasn't me what made the hurt."

"Someone else hurt you?"

Lucas again shook his head, but then apparently changed his mind and nodded, indicating yes.

"Where? Where are you hurt?" Alexandra examined his bare arms, his neck, his face, and hands then helped him sit on the examination table.

"My . . . my feelings," he said, no longer sniffling, but he dropped his head.

Alexandra felt a sickening void in her stomach. "Someone's been taunting you again, haven't they? Lucas, you must stay away from the docks. Those men can be cruel as well as ignorant."

Lucas rolled his head back and forth with vigor. "Wasn't them. And anyway it wasn't her fault. She can't help it if she died."

Alexandra placed her hand on his arm and spoke softly. "It wasn't whose fault, Lucas? Who is the *she* you speak of?"

"She's dead." His eyes filled with tears again.

"Who?" she asked again, her voice soothing.

"Blackburn's sow," he said, placing his hand over his heart. "Make it better, miss. Please." He sniffled again and gave her a pleading look.

"Oh, Lucas!" Alexandra covered his hand with hers and squeezed it before she sat down in her chair facing him. "I have no medicine to help that kind of hurt," she said.

Lucas gave her a puzzled look.

"When something or someone you love dies, it feels as if a part of you has died, too. There's nothing to do but cry and wait for the pain to go away."

He wiped his eyes with the back of a hand and gave her a look that was, oddly, wise. "I will wait," he said, then let his gaze drift as if he were staring at something in another dimension. " 'Tis heaven she's at now, ain't it?"

"Of course." Those words were the only form of medicine she could give him.

"Hog heaven," Lucas said, still staring unfocused. He didn't laugh. It was no pun he'd made. "She'll not be lonely, will she? There'll be others with her?"

"Certainly," Alexandra said. She could see that he was calmer now, but there was still sadness in his eyes.

"I got to be going now," he said. "Me mum will miss me."

Alexandra helped him down from the table. "All right, Lucas. I think you'll feel better soon, but come back again if you need to." He left without looking back, moving away with an odd lumbering skip. "And say hello to your mother," she called to him.

"A good-hearted boy, that one," Nancy said from behind her. Alexandra turned around suddenly, surprised she was there. "'Tis a pity the way some people laugh at him and call him idjet."

Alexandra barely had time to express her agreement before the next patient arrived. It was Mrs. Sommers complaining again of flatulence. The rest of the day was unremarkable with only a few patients with the usual run of minor complaints. She and Nancy went to bed early after passing the first part of the evening reading in the parlor. They were up early the next morning, Nancy busy with her housework while Alexandra made her daily rounds.

It wasn't until she saw her first patient, Hannibal Talbot, that she learned not all of Newton had passed the evening as peacefully. Ben Milligan had been found dead in a dark alley in town. His heart had been cut very neatly from his chest and then had apparently been carried away. So had the large slice of flesh that had been cut from his arm in precisely the same spot of the scar from the carbuncle that had healed.

2

Until recently, much of the gossip in Newton-Upon-Sea had been centered around what would happen to the earldom of Dunsford. Edward Boswick, fifth earl of Dunsford, had been dead a year now and, having neither siblings nor progeny, had left an unwieldy legal question as to who would succeed him. Ordinarily the heirs to aristocratic titles and holdings were of little concern to the citizens of Newton-Upon-Sea, but the late earl's country estate, which included a venerable and lovely home, was located only a few miles outside of the village. When the season ended in London each year, the house had traditionally been filled with guests from the aristocracy and the upper class for most of the summer. Their annual visits and the associated dinners and parties had been an important source of income to the merchants of Newton. Now a full season had passed without the benefit of that revenue.

The house remained empty, which meant dozens of servants had to move elsewhere to find work. Tenant farmers on the lands had remained, paying their rent to an overseer but worrying about gossip that the estate would disappear, dispersed among many heirs or sold to the highest bidder and all tenants forced off the land.

Now, even that pressing economic concern had been replaced by Ben Milligan's recent gruesome death. That was especially true in the tavern. It wasn't Alexandra's practice to frequent the Blue Ram, but she had been summoned there when Jack Sheridan, the tavern owner, accidentally cut his palm with a broken glass and was bleeding badly. It was the day after Ben's mutilated body had been found. When Alexandra arrived, she found the tavern owner seated at one of the tables, looking pale— from fright rather than from loss of blood—with his hand bandaged in a dirty bar towel stained dark with blood. He and his customers had judged the wound too serious to risk his going to the surgery himself, so one of the men had been sent to fetch her.

Alexandra saw as soon as she removed the bandage that the wound need not be serious if it could be cleaned and the bleeding stopped. She couldn't help but hear the conversation taking place at the table next to the bar as she tended Mr. Sheridan, who was called Sherry by all who knew him.

"Is it a bad un?" asked the oyster fisherman who'd been sent to fetch her. He was known to the village as Young Beaty.

"Just bring me a basin of water and some soap," she said.

The soap and water appeared quickly, and as she set about cleaning the wound, the customers lost interest and turned their conversation to another topic.

"As I wuz sayin', 'tis unnatural to cut a man's heart

out. I says 'tis the work o' the devil." Young Beaty made the pronouncement as he set his glass of beer down on the table, sloshing a little over the side. He wiped his mouth on his sleeve and nodded to reaffirm his statement. Young Beaty, at the age of forty-six, no longer fit his name, but the name had become indelibly his to distinguish him from his father, Old Beaty, who sat across from him, silent except for the slight sucking noise when he drew on his pipe.

"Devil?" said Tom Stillwell, the town's butcher, who also shared the table. "I doesn't know about devils, I doesn't, but I knows this: The man what done it knew 'is work when it comes to dressin' meat."

Old Beaty's eyes grew wide and alarmed. He pulled his pipe from his mouth and broke his silence. "Ach! Watch what yer sayin', Tom. 'Twasn't a carcass o' beef what was layin' in the alley,'twas old Ben Milligan!"

"Ain't sayin' 'twas a carcass o' beef." Tom sounded defensive. "I'm just sayin' the one what done it knew 'ow to slice meat good as any butcher." Tom glanced at Alexandra, who was now picking shards of glass from the wound. "You seen the body, mostly likely, didn't ye, Doc? And ye'll back me up. 'Twas a fine job o' slicin' what was done."

"It was brutal, Tom. That's all I can say." Alexandra pulled a needle threaded with cat gut from her bag and used it to stitch Sherry's flesh together, making an effort to concentrate on her work. She didn't want to talk about the mutilated body or even to think about it. She'd seen her share of blood and gore, of course, but there was something evil about this. The malevolence had hung in the air surrounding the body like a foul smell when she'd arrived with the constable to examine it. As for the butchering skill of the killer, Tom was right. It did show a certain amount of finesse.

"Unnatural, I says." Young Beaty turned his face away from Sherry's hand as he spoke, unwilling or unable to watch the stitching. " 'Twould have to be a madman if 'tweren't old Satan hisself."

There was a murmur of agreement.

"A lunatic!" Young Beaty's voice grew louder as he emphasized his point. "The likes o' the idjet Lucas."

Alexandra stopped her work and glanced up suddenly at the accusation. "Not Lucas! That's ridiculous." A heavy silence descended on the room as she spoke, and all eyes focused on her. "Lucas is not a madman. Not in that sense. He is simply—"

"Lucas Pendennis?" Someone at a table across the room laughed as he spoke the name in a booming voice. "A madman if I ever seen one. Thinks 'e talks to pigs, 'e does. And what's worse, 'e thinks they talks to 'im."

Where there might have otherwise been raucous laughter at such a statement, there was now only a nervous twitter, and another voice shouting, "Killed Seth Blackburn's sow, 'e did. Done it without layin' a hand on 'er. Killed 'er with black magic."

There was another twitter that quickly grew to a loud murmur, and then another voice shouting, "It ain't black magic 'e's usin', 'tis poison, but 'e's a madman just the same."

Alexandra felt a momentary void in her chest that was soon filled with dread. Blaming Lucas because of his odd behavior and deficient mental state was in itself insane. She knew him to be a gentle person who would never harm another creature intentionally.

She'd always felt protective of Lucas and of his unfortunate mother as well. Still, she knew it was true that

Lucas's behavior had become even more odd recently as he mourned the death of Blackburn's sow. He spent long hours at the pigsty and even longer hours walking around town talking to the spirit of the dead sow and assuring her there would be others of her kind to join her in heaven. That strange behavior on his part obviously helped make him a target of blame for the ungodly death and mutilation of Ben Milligan, not just in Young Beaty's mind, but in the mind of others as well. She left the tavern as soon as she could finish stitching and bandaging Sherry's hand.

It was not surprising that the hideous murder was on the minds of everyone in the three houses where Alexandra made calls the following morning. What was surprising, though, was how quickly the suspicion of Lucas Pendennis had spread and intensified. Edith Prodder, who was given to enjoying her ailments, was less concerned now about her sprained ankle than she was about the fact that Ben's body had been found in an alley very close to her house. She'd had a visit that morning from her friend Nell Stillwell, the butcher's wife, who described the killer's skill with a knife.

"Nell says her Tom could not have done a cleaner job hisself," Edith said as she lay on her bed with her foot and swollen ankle elevated on pillows. " 'Twas never a gent'ler soul than Ben Milligan, so if it could happen to the likes of him, then none o' us is safe, I say. There's a madman loose, I tell ye, and we all know who 'tis."

"Oh, do we?" Alexandra massaged tincture of camphor on Edith's ankle. "I wasn't aware Constable Snow had solved the crime."

Edith wrinkled her face in disgust. "Constable Snow? Pshaw! What does he know about solving crimes? A weaker man I never saw. And immoral, too, I suspect.

Always running off to London to visit some woman of
questionable character, I daresay."

"You've met this woman?"

"Of course not! I'm a decent woman myself." Edith
shifted her position as if to emphasize her point.

"Then how do you know—"

"How do I know? For what other reason would he be
running off to London four times a year? I know what
I'm talking about, my dear. You, being a spinster, doesn't
know about the darker side of a man's yearnings, I daresay. But mark my word, they's many a man what ought
to be married to calm the beast in 'im. Otherwise, he's
bound for the sinful life, one way or t'other." She shook
her head in disgust.

"If Constable Snow hasn't solved this crime, then who
gets the credit?" Alexandra replaced Edith's foot on the
pillows and picked up her medical bag.

"Doesn't take more than common sense to solve it, now
does it?" Edith said. "Anybody with half a mind knows
that had to be the work of a lunatic like Young Beaty
says."

Alexandra turned her head toward Edith, surprised.
"You've already heard the gossip?"

"But he's wrong about one thing, I can tell ye that,"
Edith said, ignoring the question. " 'Twasn't likely Lucas.
The boy's a pure idjet, but 'e ain't a madman, now is 'e?"

Alexandra felt a moment of relief. "Of course he's not
a madman, he's simply—"

"Borned that way, I know," Edith said, interrupting
again. " 'Tis 'is mother what's the crazy person. I says
most likely 'twas her what done it."

Alexandra dropped the bottle of camphor she'd been
trying to return to her medical bag. "Mrs. Pendennis?

Why would you say that? I've never met a saner woman in my life."

"It's *Miss,* not Mrs." Edith almost shouted her correction. "She's never entered the holy state of matrimony. Poor idjet Lucas is a bastard."

"You're right, of course. Gweneth Pendennis has never been married." Alexandra had begun to tremble. "But that doesn't make her a lunatic."

" 'Tis common knowledge, the kind of thing she done— gettin' 'erself in trouble—is symptom of a madness. A uterine disease. Makes a woman crazy. Your own father, may 'e rest in peace, was the one what told me that. Now there was a doctor for ye!"

Alexandra had become accustomed to her patients in Newton-Upon-Sea comparing her, usually unfavorably, with her late father. As for his position on the uterus and female insanity, it was true that he subscribed to the theory that female symptoms of insanity were associated with disorders of the uterus and the reproductive system. He also believed that the menstrual discharge common to all women predisposed them to insanity, since insanity was believed to be a disease of the blood. He had not, however, gone as far as the renowned London physician, Dr. Isaac Baker Brown, who routinely performed surgical removal of the clitoris as a cure for female insanity.

Yet her father would have, as Edith suggested and as Alexandra knew all too well, considered Gweneth Pendennis's indiscretion a symptom of an overly aggressive sexual appetite, which, in females, indicated insanity. On more than one occasion, he had administered leeches to the labia and cervix of women of such appetite as a treatment for female insanity.

She was also well aware that her own personality sometimes caused him concern, since strong resolve, force of character, and a certain fearlessness also were traditionally considered symptoms of insanity in women. Somehow, though, he had come to terms with these suspicious characteristics in his daughter and had eventually even encouraged them. He'd even shown a large measure of pride in her unconventional choice of a career as a doctor of medicine. She could only be thankful that he had never known the full extent of her independence.

Alexandra was grateful for all that her father had taught her about medicine, in spite of the fact that she sometimes found herself disagreeing with him. His likely diagnosis of Gweneth Pendennis, for example. Alexandra knew with certainty that one indiscretion did not mean a woman was overly sexually aggressive. But if, by chance, a woman *was* a bit aggressive in that respect, did that mean she was given to insanity? The question troubled Alexandra.

Her next stop was to check on the Blackburn boy, who had developed whooping cough. His stepmother, Helen, had taken excellent care of him, and he was recovering quickly. Enough so that Helen's concern was now less for the little boy and more for her husband's pigs, since two more besides the renowned sow had died.

"Some say the devil has cursed us." Helen's voice was choked with worry. "The devil in the body of that Pendennis boy, some say. He's always out there looking at them pigs, you know, and talking to 'em. 'Tisn't natural. He's crazy, just like his mum. People say madness is inherited."

Alexandra tried to explain that Lucas Pendennis was *not* an embodiment of the devil and that his mother was not insane, but Helen was in no mood to listen. She was far too worried about what the loss of the pigs would do to their livelihood.

Even old Mrs. Leander had heard about the murder.

She was confined to her home with severe dropsy and could hardly speak without running out of breath. Yet she was able to gasp out her fears that everyone in Newton-Upon-Sea was now in danger, and that she, herself, might expect to be murdered in her bed some night.

"Please don't worry, Mrs. Leander," Alexandra said, trying to comfort her. "You're sure to be safe here in your home. I'm certain it must have been that Ben put himself in danger by being out late at night in places you would never be."

Her words were of little comfort to the woman, however, and Alexandra knew that she would be even more difficult to comfort once the gossip about the Pendennises reached her. Yet all of Mrs. Leander's fears as well as the fears of everyone else were not without reason. The shocking details of the murder were enough to strike terror in anyone.

Having only those three patients to visit, Alexandra finished her work earlier than usual, but her concern over the murder as well as the rapidly spreading gossip left her feeling as exhausted as she might have been after seeing three times the number of patients. If the frightened mood among the villagers escalated even more, she feared Lucas and his mother's safety could be at stake.

She rode her little mare, Lucy, home as Zack followed alongside. They arrived with an hour left before Alexandra would have to open the surgery for walk-in patients. She looked forward to a few relaxing moments enjoying a quiet conversation with Nancy over lunch. Nothing would please her more than talking about something as mundane as Nancy's garden. She was quite expert at growing some of the herbs Alexandra needed for medications as well as lovely flowers and vegetables. Perhaps there would even be some beans fresh from the garden for lunch.

As soon as they entered the front door, Zack lumbered over to his favorite spot near the hearth, and Alexandra started upstairs to her room. She was partway up when she heard voices coming from the kitchen. One of the voices was Nancy's, but the other, a female voice, was not familiar. She started to ignore it, but decided to have a look, since the voice might belong to a patient whom Nancy had, for some reason, taken into the kitchen with her.

As she opened the kitchen door, it was Polly Cobbe's plump and pleasant face she saw. Polly was seated at the table with a cup of tea. She had been chatting with Nancy, who was busy stirring a pot on the stove.

Nancy turned around from the stove, a look of guilty surprise on her face. "Miss Alex! You're home early."

"Yes, I had only three patients to visit," Alexandra said, not taking her eyes off Polly. "What a pleasant surprise to see you," she said.

Polly stood quickly. "Thank you, Dr. Gladstone, but I'm sure I must be going now. Sherry was kind enough to allow me some time away, since I, too, finished my work early, but I mustn't take advantage." Her voice and manner of speaking, as Alexandra had always noticed, were refined and educated. She felt the same pang of regret that Nancy had expressed earlier, that Polly was now reduced to the job as charwoman in the Blue Ram.

"But you won't be taking advantage," Nancy insisted. "Didn't you say Sherry said you could have the entire afternoon?"

Polly looked slightly embarrassed. "Well, yes, but—"

"Please do stay," Alexandra heard herself saying, in spite of her earlier resolve for a quiet lunch with Nancy.

"It would be so pleasant to have you for luncheon."

"Oh no, I mustn't. I know you're very busy, and I—"

"Nonsense!" Nancy was already placing three plates on the table. "We'll have a nice little chat together, won't we?"

"Of course we will," Alexandra said, settling in to one of the chairs. "But we shan't talk about the murder. I've had quite enough of that for one day."

Nancy placed a cup of tea in front of her. "Of course we won't. Far too gruesome for luncheon conversation."

There was a moment of awkward silence before Alexandra spoke again. "Please, do go on with whatever your conversation was before I interrupted."

Nancy, who had seated herself next to Alexandra and across from Polly, cleared her throat nervously. "We were . . . ah, talking about the murder. I was just saying how odd the circumstances. The condition of the body, I mean. The heart missing. Truly odd."

"But of course you're right, Dr. Gladstone," Polly added. "It's hardly the proper thing for luncheon conversation."

"Indeed!" Nancy nodded her agreement with enthusiasm. "Anyway, it's plain to see how stressful 'tis been for you, Miss Alex. I'd wager it was all your patients could talk about. I suppose people think they have the awful business of the crime solved by now, and they all feel obligated to give you their opinion."

"Mmmm," Alexandra said, taking another sip of her tea and wishing they truly could get off the subject.

There was another moment of silence with no sound except silver clinking against china until Nancy could hold still no longer. "So who is the favored suspect?" she asked.

Alexandra gave her a stony look, then took a deep

breath, put down her fork, and relented. "They're saying it's the work of a madman—or woman." She glanced at Polly. "I'm sure you've heard this as well. It's all they could talk about in the Blue Ram."

"I try as best as I can to stay away from the customers and their conversations," Polly said with a sad look in her eyes.

"Of course," Alexandra said, feeling distressed.

"Anyone in particular?" the intrepid Nancy asked.

Alexandra sighed and looked at Nancy, realizing she should have expected her curiosity and insistence. "The blame appears currently to fall upon Lucas Pendennis and his mother."

"Not Miss Pendennis! And Lucas, too?" Polly sounded distressed. At the same time Nancy inhaled audibly, expressing her alarm.

"I'm afraid so," Alexandra said.

"But why?" Polly asked.

"Of course!" Nancy said before Alexandra could respond. "The murder seems so obviously the work of a madman, so they're blaming poor Lucas, who's not mad at all."

A puzzled frown creased Polly's forehead. "And neither is Miss Pendennis."

"There are those who think she is," Alexandra said after an awkward silence. "She gave birth to her son out of wedlock."

"Oh yes, of course," Polly said. "We merely laugh behind our hand at a man's indiscretions and condemn a woman to Bethlem for the same thing." Her words came out sounding more forlorn than bitter.

"I'm afraid that is sometimes the case," Alexandra said, picking up her fork and wishing again they could talk of something else.

Polly pushed her plate back, apparently having lost all interest in her meal. "What I know of Miss Pendennis leads me to believe that she is a truly virtuous woman. She is a good and loving mother and a conscientious worker. Why, practically all the customers who used to come into the apothecary always said they'd never seen finer lace than hers. And I myself know her to possess the virtues of kindness and generosity."

Nancy nodded without looking up from her plate.

"I'm afraid her one indiscretion completely ruined her reputation," Alexandra said, sawing away at the boiled meat.

"Ah yes, reputation," Polly said. "Women must mind their *reputations* more than their morality. Rather like turning attention to the show instead of the substance, isn't it?"

Alexandra turned her glance suddenly toward Polly. "You sound as if you've read Rousseau."

"What is thought of a woman is as important to her as what she really is," Nancy, who had also read Rousseau, quoted.

"Important to her because it is important to others," Polly said. "We should never have heard of Lucretia had she died to preserve her virtue instead of her reputation."

"We have a bluestocking amongst us!" Alexandra said, both amused and pleased.

"I have not always been a charwoman," Polly said.

"And so should you not be now!" Nancy sounded agitated.

Polly breathed a resigned sigh. "I assumed Mr. Neill's apprentice would always be there to carry on at the apothecary and there'd be no need for me to look elsewhere for work."

"Clyde Wright?" Nancy rolled her eyes. "That ne're-

do-well? Some nerve he had, leaving in the middle of the
night without notice. You're better off not working for
him."

"I can't say I'm certain of that," Polly said. "I only
know that decent positions are rare in Newton-Upon-Sea.
I have a small savings from my employment at the apothecary, but not enough, I'm afraid, to get me to London to
find suitable work. My hope is to save enough at my current job."

Alexandra didn't fail to catch the glance, fraught with
meaning, Nancy threw at her. She might have been forced
to embarrass herself and Polly as well by having to admit
she could not afford to offer her enough work to sustain
her, had not the bell on the surgery door rung.

It was Lucas Pendennis. He was carrying something
bloody and encrusted with dirt. It looked very much like
a human heart, and behind him his mother cried uncontrollably.

3

Constable Robert Snow preferred to stand when he questioned a prisoner or a suspect, whom he always made sure was seated. Perhaps it was a carryover from the days when he had been the schoolmaster in Newton-Upon-Sea. He had learned then that his substantial height could be even more intimidating if he made the misbehaving student sit while he towered over him. It was not that Constable Snow was fond of intimidation, but he was most certainly fond of·order and discipline.

He had never in his career, either as a teacher or an officer of the law, had to deal with a half-wit, however. Lucas Pendennis, the stocky, dark-haired boy who sat in front of him now, was testimony to the fact that he lacked the skill to question such a person effectively. Dr. Gladstone waited quietly in one of the chairs to his left, and beside her, sobbing uncontrollably, was the boy's mother, a petite woman with hair the color of corn silk and eyes like deep blue lakes. It was Dr. Gladstone who had

brought the boy and his mother to his office, along with
some putrid-smelling thing that sat in a crockery bowl
covered with a linen towel on his desk.

He was very much aware of Dr. Gladstone's scrutiny
of him as he spoke to Lucas. It gave him an odd feeling
to know that she was assessing his skills, especially since,
in the past, it had been he who was charged with assessing
hers. When he was still a schoolmaster, her father and his
good friend, the late Dr. Huntington Gladstone, had hired
him as a tutor for his daughter, since, quite naturally, being female, she was not allowed to attend school. Gladstone had also allowed his daughter's young companion
and servant, Nancy, to sit in on the lessons.

"Very well, Lucas," Snow said, doing his best to ignore
Dr. Gladstone's careful attention as well as the other
woman's sobs. "You have told me you found the organ
buried in the ground. . . ."

Lucas gave him a blank look.

Snow pointed to the crockery. "That." The one word
sounded condescending, rather than full of exaggerated
patience, as he had intended.

Lucas nodded his head enthusiastically. "Oh yes. I
found it where the truffles is." He sat very straight in his
chair, unlike Snow's usual suspects or former students,
who usually cowered in fear.

"Yes, among the truffles. Now tell me, please, what led
you to excavate that specific area?"

Lucas gave Snow a slack-jawed stare for several seconds before he turned his gaze to his mother, this time
with a puzzled expression.

It was Dr. Gladstone who spoke to him, however, since
his mother's quiet sobs made it impossible for her to
speak. "Why were you digging there, Lucas?" Dr. Gladstone kept her voice low and her tone gentle.

" 'Cause," Lucas said, speaking to Dr. Gladstone.

"Because of what?" she said, coaxing him, still with gentleness.

Lucas shrugged and looked at the ceiling.

Snow felt a stab of impatience mingled with despair, but he pushed his emotions aside, determined to accomplish his goal. "Did you know it was there, Lucas?"

"What?" Lucas said, still looking at the ceiling.

Snow's spine grew involuntarily tense, but he forced himself to relax. "The organ you excava—the organ you dug out of the ground. That one." Snow pointed again to the bowl on his desk. "The one you brought to Dr. Gladstone."

"That?" Lucas asked, also pointing to the bowl.

"Yes, Lucas."

"That's a heart. It ain't no organ, 'tis a heart."

"Of course." The long, well-tapered fingers of Snow's hands met under his chin as he looked down at Lucas's face.

" 'Tis a heart, and I'm going to keep it." Lucas spoke emphatically, but his gaze drifted about the room.

His mother stopped her sobbing and stared at him, her eyes wide with horror.

"Lucas, look at me, please." Snow's voice shook slightly from the strain of forced patience. When Lucas turned his eyes toward him, he continued. "Whose heart is it?" Lucas ignored his question and stood up suddenly, going toward the table, his hands extended toward the crockery. Snow grabbed his arm, restraining him. Dr. Gladstone and the boy's mother, both alarmed, stood as well.

"Let me go!" Lucas said, struggling. "It's mine! I found it, so it's mine!"

"How did you know it was there?" Snow asked.

"Lucas!" Miss Pendennis cried before he could answer. She reached for her son, but Dr. Gladstone held her back.

At the same time Lucas spoke. "I put it there! That's how I knowed. It's mine, and I can do what I want with it!"

There was an anguished cry from Miss Pendennis, and Snow's breath came in short gasps, which he had to control in order to speak. "You put it there?" His mind was reeling. Was it going to be that easy to solve the case? Would a half-wit's confession hold up under the law?

"The boy doesn't understand, Constable Snow," Dr. Gladstone said, still holding on to Miss Pendennis, who once again was wailing.

"Please sit down, ladies," Snow had to shout to be heard above the noise. When he saw that both women had obeyed him and that Dr. Gladstone had managed to quiet the hysterical woman once more, he turned back to Lucas. "Listen to me carefully, Lucas. I want you to tell me how you got the org—the heart in the first place."

Lucas stared at him, uncomprehending.

"Where did you get the heart?" Snow said again, enunciating each word.

"Out of here," Lucas said, pointing to his chest.

"Out of your own chest?"

Lucas laughed and looked down at his intact chest.

"Lucas!" Snow spoke sharply to get the boy's attention and to distract him from his laughter. It worked. The boy's eyes locked onto his own. "You would have to cut that heart out of a person. Is that how you got it? Did you cut it out?"

Lucas's eyes became unfocused for a moment as if he had moved his soul to another location, but he slowly rejoined himself and brought his attention back to Snow. "Yes," he said, nodding his head. "I think so."

"Did you cut it from the body of Ben Milligan?"

Snow's words went unheard as Miss Pendennis's keening filled the room and frightened Lucas so much that he ran to her and encircled her with his arms.

"I'm sorry, Mum. I won't do it again," he said.

"Surely you know this boy hasn't the skill for such an expert surgery," Dr. Gladstone said in the same instant.

Snow ignored her and watched the boy and his mother, overwhelmed for a moment by the need to walk away. A mother's grief was never easy for him to witness, and the very sordid nature of this entire case was repulsive to him. This was not the sort of thing he'd expected when he traded his life as a schoolmaster for that of a constable. And this was not the first time he wondered if he had made the right decision, until he reminded himself of the reason he had taken the position. The higher salary was attractive, especially given his constant and increasing need for more money.

"Miss Pendennis," he said, forcing any sign of emotion from his voice and steeling himself for her response. "I shall have to place your son under arrest." There, he had said it, and the woman was yawling as Dr. Gladstone did her best to comfort her while she continued to protest that the boy did not have the skills. He closed his eyes for a brief moment, knowing the unpleasantness would pass, knowing, too, that he had done his duty. After all, he as good as had a confession from the boy. The courts would decide whether or not he was capable of the removal. Whether he was or not, it was highly likely his mental state would keep him from the gallows. He would go to an asylum, where he would be better off, and his mother would adjust to his absence. Women were resilient in that way. Perhaps the boy's temporary incarceration in the gaol would be best at the moment anyway, given the frightened mood of the citizenry. Snow was well aware that most of them blamed the insane act on the poor im-

becile. He knew, too, that a select few even targeted his
unfortunate mother.

In Snow's mind, there was no need to consider her a
suspect, since he had one in hand who had made a confession and who had provided circumstantial evidence as
well. He would not consider the mother even in the light
of her alleged madness. The common malady of so-called
uterine insanity, with which she was said to be cursed,
was something he knew little of and, further, preferred
not to know.

He was happy to see that Dr. Gladstone was adminis-
tering to the woman, offering her comforting words as
well as the contents of some mysterious vial she had
pulled from her bag. He was dismayed, however, when,
just as he was leading a confused but docile Lucas away,
Dr. Gladstone called out to him.

"Yes, Doctor," he said, turning to face her.

"Surely you know, sir, that Lucas's confession means
nothing. He doesn't understand what is happening, and I
daresay that, under the right circumstances, he would con-
fess to murdering the queen."

"I am well aware of the prisoner's mental state, Dr.
Gladstone," Snow said, keeping his tone of voice well
controlled. "There is certainly reason to expect that the
amount of responsibility that is exacted from him under
the law will not be comparable to that of a sane person."

"You are judging him guilty without benefit of due process."

He remembered now how, as a student, she could
sometimes be rather trying with her constant challenging.
"I am neither judge nor jury, Miss Alexandra. My judgment extends only to the point of reasonable suspicion.
My judgment also requires me to consider the safety of
the suspect." He was aware that he had used the form of
address for her he had used when she was his student,

rather than her well-earned title of doctor. He did not apologize or attempt to correct himself, however, in spite of the fact that he could see in her eyes that she expected it.

He saw her hesitate for a moment before she spoke. "If you are considering Lucas's well-being, then surely you know incarceration is seldom conducive to health." It was a brave attempt, but her voice sounded considerably less self-assured. She was obviously aware of the need for Lucas's safety as well as he. That brief betrayal of weakness gave him the opportunity for the last word.

"And surely your profession has taught you that what is or is not conducive to one's health or well-being is sometimes a matter of degree." He grasped Lucas's arm and led him through the doorway to the gaol.

Alexandra saw Gweneth Pendennis to her home and gave her laudanum as a sedative, then stayed with her until she was asleep. It would take more than laudanum to ease her distress permanently, however. She would need reassurance that Lucas would not be harmed and could be returned safely to her. Alexandra left, planning to return early the next morning. She was not at all certain how she would manage to reassure her in light of the undeniably grim prospects for the boy.

It was very late when she returned to her house, yet she was not at all surprised to see a light burning in the parlor—a sign that Nancy was still awake and waiting for her. She would want to know everything that had happened. It was just as well, Alexandra thought, since sleep would not come easily for her now.

Neither Nancy nor Zack greeted her as she opened the front door, a fact that surprised her. She knew the reason

as soon as she stepped into the parlor. Polly Cobbe was
still there, seated on one of the damask settees while Zack
rested his head in her lap and Nancy sat across from her.
It might have been an altogether pleasant and cozy scene
had it not been for Polly's pale face and the frightened
look in her eyes.

"What a pleasant surprise to find you still here," Alexandra said.

"I asked her to stay." Nancy's voice had a note of de-
fensiveness. "As you can imagine, she's quite upset as a
result of all that's—"

"Forgive me." Polly pushed Zack's head from her lap
and stood. "Nancy has been so very kind, and she's right,
of course, I am upset, but I know I must be going. I have
my work tomorrow. But first," she added, "please do tell
me what happened with young Lucas."

Alexandra slumped into a chair, feeling suddenly exhausted. "I'm afraid young Lucas is in gaol."

Nancy sprang to her feet. "I was afraid of that! Some
people can be so terribly narrow-minded!"

Polly shook her head in disbelief. "That can't be. Surely
no one can believe he would—"

"Unfortunately, he as much as confessed." Alexandra's
voice sounded weary even to her own ears.

"Confessed?" Polly looked troubled. "No, not Lucas!
He's an imbecile. No one will believe a confession from
him!" She'd grown quite agitated.

Alexandra stood instinctively to comfort her. "You're
right, of course." She placed an arm around her shoulder.
"The poor boy had no idea to what he was confessing.
One would hope the courts will take his mental condition
into consideration."

"To what end?" Polly seemed near tears. "To be found
guilty, but his life spared only to live out a miserable life
in an asylum?"

"Is there no hope that his confession will be discounted?" Nancy asked.

"There is always hope," Alexandra said without much conviction. She dropped her arm from Polly's shoulder with a sigh. "But it would take a barrister with uncommon skill to accomplish that, the likes of which I'm afraid—"

"The likes of Nicholas Forsythe of London," Nancy said.

"We know very little of Mr. Forsythe's expertise in these matters," Alexandra said.

"He's the only barrister we know." Nancy was emphatic.

"Hardly a recommendation."

At the same time Polly asked, "Who is Nicholas Forsythe?"

Nancy opened her mouth to explain, but Alexandra interrupted her before she could say a word and reveal more detail about Mr. Forsythe than was necessary.

"A London barrister whose acquaintance I made a year or so ago when he was visiting the late earl of Dunsford at his country estate here."

"I know the place," Polly said. "A rather grand country house about four miles from Newton."

"Precisely," Alexandra said.

Polly gave her a curious frown. "And I gather you doubt the capabilities of this Mr. Forsythe."

"I don't doubt him at all," Alexandra said a little too defensively. "It is simply that I am not privy to his reputation except on a very limited scale." She was dismayed to find herself blushing. "To contact him seems impractical anyway. As you know, it would take some time to get a letter to London requesting his services, and then, of course, even more time for him to arrange his schedule to travel here."

"There is always the telegraph," Nancy said, which

made Alexandra glare at her. Alexandra was not certain why she was working so hard at keeping Mr. Forsythe away, except that his combination of masculinity and boyish charm sometimes made her feel as flustered as a schoolgirl.

"The telegraph. Of course," Alexandra managed to say, in spite of her chagrin. "Perhaps I should take advantage of that." She was admittedly slow at adapting to modern technology.

"Certainly we must do something to keep the poor boy from accepting the blame." Polly sounded accusative, as if she thought Alexandra's reluctance was directed against helping Lucas.

"Of course you're right," she said, chastened. "I shall write the message out, and Nancy can see that it's transmitted first thing in the morning."

"Oh yes!" Nancy said. Her enthusiasm, for some reason, made Alexandra uneasy.

"Very well," she said, trying to push her unease aside. "And since we all have work to do tomorrow, I suggest we all go to bed and try to get as much rest as possible." She turned to Polly. "I also suggest you stay here, Polly. We all three know the killer is still out there, and it's not advisable for you to be out so late alone."

"Oh, but I couldn't . . ."

"You can have my father's room for the night," Alexandra said before the woman could protest more.

Polly seemed in no mood to protest with any earnestness, however. She acquiesced easily, and they were soon all three upstairs in separate rooms. Alexandra found it difficult to sleep at first, and when she did sleep, Zack, who always slept on the floor beside her bed, woke her once with a nervous bark, as if he'd had a bad dream. She was able to quiet him only by allowing him to sprawl his massive form on her bed, covering her feet.

4

Alexandra was dressed and downstairs by six the next morning, knowing she needed to get an early start. Besides her usual rounds to visit her patients and her surgery hours to keep, there were certain tasks of pharmacology she must see to, now that there was no longer an apothecary to rely upon. As she entered the kitchen, Zack following closely behind, she was surprised to see Nancy and Polly already there, chattering and laughing like two schoolgirls as they crushed herbs, each with mortar and pestle. Several pots bubbled on the stove.

"You're both up early," Alexandra said as she entered the kitchen.

Nancy glanced up. "Good morning, miss. I thought it best I get an early start on the mixtures we can store without worry of spoilage. We need to have them in stock, you know, since the apothecary closed. Poor Mr. Neill." Her face was flushed, due, perhaps, to both the heat of the kitchen and her pleasure at having Polly as company.

"And you're up rather early yourself, if you don't mind my saying so."

It was clear Nancy was on her best behavior since, under ordinary circumstances, she openly spoke her mind without giving much thought to what Alexandra might think. In spite of her father's frequent expressions of concern at the close and, in his opinion, overly friendly relationship between the two of them, Alexandra had long ago stopped worrying about the propriety of their relationship as servant and mistress.

"Yes, I am up early," Alexandra said, helping herself to a cup of tea. "I had in mind the same thing, to get some of our staple medicines prepared ahead of time, but I see I'm a little late."

"Polly's been a great help." Nancy spoke as she poured diluted alcohol into the powdery mixture she'd created in the bowl.

"Yes, I can see that." Alexandra stirred her tea as she glanced at Polly. "You seem quite adept, Polly. I can see that Mr. Neill taught you well."

Polly nodded. "Oh yes, he relied upon me occasionally to help him with some of the more simple tasks. He left the difficult ones to Clyde. He was a good apprentice, that one."

"Humff!" Nancy said with a shake of her head. "May have been a good apprentice, but he's lecherous as a goat and lacking in sense, if you ask me. Running off the way he did just when he was about to become a full-fledged apothecary."

"He can be rather disgustingly lecherous, I suppose," Polly said. "But he's young. Not quite ripe, you might say. There's always hope he'll change." Polly handed her bowl with its crushed herbs to Nancy to add the alcohol.

"And I have to admit it was odd that he left so suddenly. Except . . ."

"Except what?" Nancy prompted.

"I don't want to be a gossip . . ."

"Polly!" Nancy was playfully scolding.

"Well, there did seem to be some funds missing just as he . . ." She waved a hand. "There's no proof he took them. Forgive me." She turned to Alexandra. "I do wish I could stay and help more, just to show how much I appreciate your letting me stay last night. But I must be going now. Can't afford to lose another position."

"Of course not." Alexandra set her teacup aside. "And it was a pleasure to have—" A sudden knock at the surgery door and Zack's almost immediate bark interrupted her. They both knew what it meant. Someone had arrived with an emergency.

She hurried to the surgery door and opened it to find a young man of no more than twenty years holding an infant in his arms. The infant, whom she estimated to be a few months less than a year old, appeared to be choking. Her face had turned blue and there was a stream of blood flowing from her nose. Behind the man and the baby, a girl of perhaps sixteen, who must have been the mother, tried, with little success, to stifle her own sobs and tears. Alexandra reached for the child and called to the parents over her shoulder. "How long has she been like this?"

"She's sick, miss," the young father said, apparently too upset to answer Alexandra's question. "Coughing. Not breathing . . . My wife . . . You've got to help us, please, miss. Our baby . . . We cannot . . ." The young man's voice shook as he stuttered, and he seemed about to give in to tears himself.

It was obvious to Alexandra that she was not likely to get information of any value from either of them. She turned into the room, holding the baby, vaguely aware of both Polly and Nancy standing close by. She immediately placed a finger into the baby's throat, bringing out a roapy mass of thick mucus. A high-pitched, almost inhuman noise escaped her tiny throat as she attempted a deep intake of breath. When she coughed again and the cough continued, alternating with the awful noise, Alexandra could see both young parents' eyes widen in fear as they clutched each other. She had no time to reassure them, however, since the baby had stopped breathing again.

"Infusion of red clover blossoms?" Nancy asked, already on her way to the kitchen storage shelf to retrieve the proper vial. Polly, in the meantime, was busy with something behind her.

"Yes," Alexandra said to Nancy, "but first . . ." She stopped speaking and placed her mouth on the blue lips of the infant in an attempt to supply her with breath. Still the child did not breathe, and she tried again. When there was still no breath, she glanced up and shouted for Nancy. In the next instant, Polly had taken the baby from her and was wrapping her in a sheet. Alexandra had no time to ask how she knew what had to be done. Instead she reached for a linen-covered tray on which Nancy kept her surgical instruments boiled and ready for use. She was surprised to find that the correct size of silver tube had already been attached to the introducer she needed. A thin silk thread dangled from the end of the tube. She glanced at Polly, realizing that was what she had been doing behind her.

She saw that Polly already had the baby wrapped tightly in the blanket to keep her from moving and was holding her upright against her own body, facing outward. Nancy, who had returned to the surgery, helped hold the baby's head against Polly's chest.

Alexandra passed the introducer and tube into the throat and larynx. She was vaguely aware of the parents huddled together and deathly quiet in a corner of the room. Carefully and slowly she removed the introducer from the baby's throat while she held the tube in place with her index finger. When the instrument was completely removed, Nancy tied the silk thread behind the baby's head to hold the tube in place while Alexandra turned toward the frightened parents.

"You must leave the tube in awhile to help the baby breathe, and you must watch her carefully," she said.

The young mother hardly seemed to be listening. Her eyes were on the baby, whom Polly had now unwrapped and was cradling in her arms. She rocked her back and forth and spoke to her in soothing tones to hush her hoarse crying.

The baby's crying served only to frighten the young mother even more. "What's wrong with her?"

"Whooping cough," Polly said before Alexandra could answer. "It affects the smallest ones worse, their breathing passages being small. But see, she's breathing now." The baby's cries were beginning to subside to a hoarse whimper, and Polly handed her to the mother. "Careful now, don't disturb the tube," she said as she transferred her from her own arms to her mother's. "You must keep her quiet. Any excitement will start her cough again." While the mother held her, Polly rubbed the little girl's plump cheek gently with the backs of her fingers and spoke to the mother, still in her soft, soothing voice. "A teaspoon of the infusion of red clover the doctor will give you will help modify the irritation in her passages." As she turned away toward Alexandra, she was suddenly and acutely embarrassed. "I . . . I'm sorry," she said. "I didn't mean to—"

"Please. Don't apologize." Alexandra spoke quietly to avoid disturbing the baby. She glanced at the child, breathing noisily through the tube and growing drowsy in her mother's arms. "I appreciate your help; you seem quite experienced."

"My younger sister had whooping cough when she was an infant. I nursed her through it. And of course, having worked in the apothecary shop, I learned a bit about medication." Polly also spoke in hushed tones, but she looked down, still embarrassed. "But in this case I overstepped the bounds. You are the doctor, of course."

Nancy picked up the bottle containing the infusion of clover and handed it to the parents then signaled Polly with her eyes, and the two of them left the room, leaving Alexandra alone with the young family.

Both parents were much calmer now, but they huddled together still, the young man peering over his wife's shoulder at their sleeping child. As Alexandra approached them, the mother glanced up at her, and she could see the fear still in her eyes. "She breathes ragged." Her voice was still high-pitched, like a little girl's.

"Shhh," Alexandra said, watching the baby's labored breathing. The cough was quiet, at least for the moment, and she was no longer blue from lack of oxygen. "She will likely have more coughing spells," Alexandra whispered. "You must watch her carefully."

The young girl gave her a frightened look, but didn't speak. Her husband had now grown quite pale and looked as if he might faint.

"Is your home far from here?" Alexandra asked. Although she had helped birth most of the babies in Newton, she didn't recognize this young couple. They were undoubtedly new laborers for the earl's estate.

The girl shook her head. "No more than half a mile,"

she said, also whispering. "On Earl's Row. Third cottage on the chapel side." The boy seemed unable to respond.

Alexandra nodded. Earl's Row was a small cluster of one- and two-room cottages where farm laborers who worked on the lands owned by the earl of Dunsford lived, and it was, indeed, no more than half a mile away, a ten-minute walk perhaps. The chapel side meant the same side of the street on which the Methodist chapel stood. "I think you can safely take the baby home," Alexandra said, "but keep her quiet and in a darkened room if possible so she won't be stimulated. Stimulation will make her cough, and she could choke again. Also keep her away from other children. The disease is quite contagious. Do you have other children?"

The girl shook her head again.

"Good." She reached to give the girl a reassuring pat on her shoulder. "I'll send Nancy with you to help you watch, and then I shall stay with her tonight, since she is likely to be worse in the night air. Remember, the cough will last for several weeks and beware of the choking."

The girl nodded and gave her a smile that was part fear and part gratitude before she turned toward the door with her husband beside her and the baby in her arms.

"Wait!" Alexandra called to their backs. "I don't know your names."

The girl turned back to face her and spoke in her little-girl voice. "Kate Hastings. And Jim," she added as an afterthought.

"And the babe?"

"Alice."

"You still put her to breast?"

Kate nodded. "But she won't suckle."

"She will suckle when she can breathe. Nancy can re-move the tube in an hour or two, and you must try to get

her to suckle as much as possible. Her body needs the
fluids."

Again Kate nodded before she turned away with her
small family to begin their walk back to their cottage.
Alexandra watched them go, wishing she could have sent
them away with a reassuring word. The truth, however,
was that whooping cough in an infant below the age of a
year was extremely dangerous.

When they had gone, she went to the kitchen to join
Nancy and Polly. She wanted to make certain Nancy had
a good supply of the infusion of red clover flowers, since
there was likely to be more cases of whooping cough, in
spite of all attempts to avoid the spread. She found Nancy
alone in the kitchen. She was filling the last of the vials
with one of the various concoctions she had mixed earlier.

"You'll be sending me to stay with the babe," she said.

"Yes, but finish your breakfast first. Has Polly left?"
Alexandra asked as she went to the larder for a loaf of
the bread Nancy had baked the day before. She also took
the bowl of butter Nancy had left sitting in a pan of water
to keep it cool.

"Polly's gone to her work at the tavern." Nancy used
her apron to wipe the moisture from the last bottle she
had filled.

Alexandra cut two thick slices of the bread and placed
one on a plate for her and the second on a plate for Nancy.
"I must say she proved quite efficient in an emergency."
She regretted it immediately. It would only provide an
opening for more pressure from Nancy to hire her, and
she would no doubt augment her argument with the fact
that she was equally adept at preparing medicines.

"Says she learned it caring for her sister," Nancy said.
"Not the same as being properly trained as an assistant
by a doctor, now is it?"

Alexandra glanced at her, surprised. "Why Nancy, if I didn't know better, I'd say you were jealous of Polly's skills."

"And why should I be?" Nancy's tone was a bit too sharp.

"Why indeed," Alexandra said. She was surprised at Nancy's sudden turn toward jealousy after being so keen to hire her. Perhaps seeing the woman's efficiency made her feel threatened. It was just as well, though, to have the pressure for hiring her removed, since it would be financially difficult. Perhaps, though, she could find employment for Polly at Bradfordshire Hospital. Many hospitals still hired nurses who had not been formally trained. Women like Polly often resisted the job, however, since nurses too often came from the ranks of prostitutes. Still, it might bear investigating. Alexandra helped herself to another slice of bread. "This is wonderful, Nancy. Do you have a new recipe? And what is that wonderful smell?"

Nancy was slow to respond, still apparently distracted. "Oh," she said finally, "the smell? It's mutton. Or leg of lamb, as Polly calls it. It's roasting in the oven, can you imagine? Roasting when it could be boiled just as well? Polly insisted she show me how, so she rubbed it with some of the herbs, browned it in oil, and put it in the oven. Not a drop of water, either. But don't worry, I've saved a bit for boiling in case you don't like it."

They had finished their breakfast, and Alexandra was about to leave the house for her morning calls when she heard a knock at the front door. Nancy gave her a quick glance, obviously as surprised as she was that the knock had come at the front door and not the surgery. Alexandra was not far behind her when Nancy opened the door to Constable Snow. Beside him, looking pale and visibly trembling, stood Polly Cobbe.

Snow was the first to speak. "Forgive me for troubling
you so early in the morning, Dr. Gladstone, but I must
ask you to come with me."

"Of course," Alexandra said, reaching for her bag,
but—"

"I'm afraid there's been another murder."

"Another murder? Who?" Nancy asked.

"I'm afraid we don't have a name." Snow's voice was
unusually grave. "A stranger from the lower strata of society, apparently, and rather down on his luck, I'd say.
Miss Cobbe found the body in the alley behind the Blue
Ram. Quite close to where Ben Milligan was found."

"Oh my lord, Polly! Was he . . . ?" Nancy appeared too
aghast to continue, but Snow answered nevertheless.

"The same unsavory circumstances, I'm afraid." He
turned his gaze back to Alexandra. "Unfortunately I must
ask you once again to examine the body."

"Of course," Alexandra said, already on her way out
the door.

"And Polly, you must stay here!" Nancy said, moving
toward her, apparently no longer miffed. "You must be
quite in shock!"

Polly could respond with nothing more than a dull
stare, as if something had drowned in the deep wells that
were her eyes, but Snow answered sharply, "I shall have
to ask Miss Cobbe to come with me for questioning."

"Begging you pardon, sir. Can't you see she's—"

"That will be quite enough, Nancy!" Snow's tone was
even sharper. He was not as indulgent of Nancy's imper-
tinence as was Alexandra.

Nancy lowered her head. "Of course, sir. Forgive me,
sir." To see Nancy acting like an ordinary servant gave
Alexandra a momentary shock, but she couldn't dwell

upon it. She could sense the urgency in Snow's demeanor and knew they must be on their way.

It was a short ride in the constable's carriage to the alley behind the Blue Ram. Alexandra sat facing Polly all the way, watching her pale face and her empty eyes. She inquired of her once whether she was all right. Polly jerked her gaze toward her as if she was startled and replied with one whispered word, "Yes."

It was not surprising to Alexandra that Polly was in shock. Having seen the other body herself, she knew how brutal and disturbing the scene most likely was. Snow stopped his carriage a few feet away from the lifeless form lying in a pool of blood in the narrow alley. Polly made no move to step down from the carriage when Snow got down from his perch and opened the door. She simply stared straight ahead, still pale but no longer trembling.

Alexandra took the constable's proffered hand as she stepped from the carriage. As soon as she saw the body, she understood more clearly Polly's near catatonic state. The man's chest had been brutally mutilated. The flesh on each side of the rib cage had been sliced, as it had been on the other victim. But this time, the cuts were not the clean surgical cuts she'd seen before. Instead they were ragged and messy. The severed ribs were also jagged and uneven, unlike the precision work done on the other man. It was as if the killer had been in a hurry. The heart had been removed as before, but there was evidence of tearing of the surrounding tissue, rather than the precise surgical removal she'd seen on the first victim. As further testimony of the killer's haste, bits of the flesh lay a few feet away, coated in dust and dried blood, as if it had been carelessly flung aside. The heart, like Ben's, was missing.

As Alexandra examined the body, she noticed the same purplish color of the skin and the same pale lips and nails she'd seen on Ben Milligan's body. However, unlike the other victim, there were no maggots present, and the limbs were blue. He had been dead no more than an hour.

Before she finished the examination, a small crowd gathered, and in spite of Snow's stern commands that everyone stay back, the group moved closer and closer as if it were one body.

A faceless voice cried out from somewhere. " 'Tis that idjet Lucas again! See what 'e done. None 'o us is safe!"

"Yer the idjet," a deep, resounding voice shouted. "The boy's in gaol. Even a sane man couldn't do this from inside a lockup."

"The bastard's mum's the one what done it, I say," someone else said, a woman this time. "She's not right in the 'ead either, you know. The boy inherited it from her, if you ask me."

"Who says she ain't right in the 'ead?" the deep voice said again.

If there was an answer to that question, it was impossible to tell, because the crowd grew too noisy to distinguish one voice from another. Alexandra knew, though, that the old argument of Gweneth Pendennis's sexual indiscretion being linked to insanity was in full swing, along with a dangerous level of fear mixed with anger.

Constable Snow had little patience for the rabble's noise or judgments, however. He raised his voice, which was remarkably strong for one so thin, and ordered the crowd dispersed. They obeyed, but reluctantly. Alexandra could feel the fear emanating from the many-headed beast as it moved away. There were threatening shouts thrown at Snow for not having already captured the mad killer and put him or her in gaol. It also occurred to Alexandra that it was likely a female would not have been considered at all, had it not been for the fact that Gweneth Pendennis had two strikes against her. She'd borne an idiot son and she'd borne him out of wedlock.

When the crowd was dispersed, or more accurately, reassembled in another place, Snow had the body transported to Percy Gibbs's funeral parlor for Alexandra to examine further. He ordered Polly to accompany him back to his office so he could question her.

"Perhaps the questioning could wait," Alexandra said, seeing that Polly's face had grown even paler and that she had become more agitated. The crowd had undoubtedly upset her. Alexandra thought she might faint or burst into tears.

She did neither, however. Instead, she spoke quietly but in a voice that still trembled. "No, no, we mustn't wait. I don't want them to blame that poor woman. How could they think she could—"

"I shan't keep Miss Cobbe long, but it is imperative that I get an official statement as to how she came to find the body." Snow's voice was cold, as if he resented having to justify his actions.

"Are you quite certain you'll be all right, Miss Cobbe?" Alexandra said. "Perhaps I could send Nancy over to stay with—?"

"Please, don't trouble her. I'll be quite all right." Her bravery and confidence seemed forced.

"Very well," Alexandra said, deciding not to pressure her but resolving to stop by the tavern later to check on her.

When she reached the funeral parlor and began to examine the body, she confirmed the conclusion she'd reached earlier. He had apparently been attacked from behind, and his two carotid arteries severed with a very sharp knife. Then his chest was cut open to reveal the rib cage. The ribs, as before, were snipped on each side and pulled away so the heart could be surgically removed, this time with less care and precision. She had just completed her examination when she heard the muffled sound of the crowd again.

She ran through the work room to the parlor at the front of the building, still wearing her bloodstained apron, to peer out the window. She was met there by Mr. and Mrs. Gibbs, who had heard the noise too.

"What is it?" Mrs. Gibbs asked.

The voice of the crowd had intensified and was even angrier and more fear-crazed. Then, a single scream full of terror resonated over all the other voices, giving Mrs. Gibbs her answer. Alexandra leaned forward to peer through the window into the street. What she saw sickened her. Gweneth Pendennis was being dragged by her arms, facedown, along the street.

5

As soon as Alexandra could rid herself of her apron and
gloves, she rushed into the street, calling to the crowd to
let the woman go. With Zack running beside her, barking
feverishly, she rushed to Gweneth's aid but was rudely
pushed aside. She landed on her backside in the dust of
the street. Had she not been quickly pulled to her feet and
moved, somewhat roughly, out of the way, she might have
been trampled by the crowd. It took her a moment to
realize it was Polly who had rescued her. Zack stood by
encouraging her with his bark.

"They're mad! All of them!" Polly cried. "We've got
to stop them from harming that woman."

Alexandra forgot about Zack as she rushed ahead with
Polly, both of them trying to reach Gweneth. They made
little headway through the mob, which moved as slow as
clotted blood, carrying its hate like a disease into the heart
of the town. Then suddenly the crowd stopped any forward movement, pooling in confused eddies and washing

back on itself. Constable Snow, mounted on his horse, was in front of the rabble shouting for order.

It was impossible to hear his words, but the sound carried authority, enough to turn the tide. Up ahead she saw Gweneth struggle to her feet, and someone, a man, hoisted her onto the back of Snow's horse, where she leaned against him like a lifeless rag doll. By this time the noise of the horde had lessened enough to hear Snow's angry threats. . .

". . . or all of you will face the gallows! Remember you are British citizens, not barbarians. And everyone, this woman included, is innocent until proven guilty! Go, I said! All of you!"

Alexandra had never seen him so angry. There was another angry, frightened shout from the crowd. "They's a killer amongst us and yer doin' nothin' about it!" That brought a rumble of fear and anger that surged dangerously toward Snow, but he pulled something from inside his coat, and there was a loud explosion. Alexandra had never known Snow to carry a gun, and it appeared the one he had pulled from his coat was an old-fashioned dueling pistol.

"Get back, damn you! All of you!" he shouted, with his now impotent pistol no longer aimed upward, but pointed at the simmering mass. There was a moment of stunned stillness. Snow shouted again, and the crowd stirred, stumbling over itself as each individual tried to turn or back away. Snow waited, his pistol still aimed and with a pale and frightened Gweneth clinging to him, until he was certain the angry confluence had evaporated into homes and alleyways and shops. Only Alexandra and Polly remained, along with Zack. Alexandra felt herself trembling and sensed that Polly was trembling as well.

"Go home, both of you," Snow said, returning his pistol

to an inside pocket of his coat. "And don't worry, I'll see that Miss Pendennis and her son are not harmed."

Constable Snow started to turn his horse, but something caught his eye and caused him to hesitate at the same time Zack barked twice and tensed his body. When Alexandra turned her gaze in the direction of Snow's, she saw someone, a male of slight build, who seemed to be lurking in the shadow of a building. He apparently realized he'd attracted attention, however, and disappeared in the narrow space between two shops. Snow, satisfied that there would be no more trouble, turned and rode away with Gweneth, who was still too frightened to speak.

"That was . . ." Polly spoke in a whisper, and when Alexandra turned toward her, she saw a troubled frown on the woman's face as she stared at the space between the two buildings where the mysterious figure had disappeared. "That was Clyde," she said, still whispering.

"Clyde Wright?" Alexandra asked. "The apprentice?"

Polly shook her head. "I can't be certain, but it looked rather like him."

"Do you suppose he's returned, thinking he'll get his old position back?"

"Well," Polly said, wearing a troubled expression, "even if Mr. Neill was still alive, he wouldn't take on young Clyde as an apprentice again. That young man ruined his chances, running off as he did, without so much as a by-your-leave at the same time the money disappeared." She shook her head. "One can never really know what another person will do."

"I suppose not," Alexandra said, glancing around uneasily. There was an odd taint of danger still in the air.

"I must go," Polly said, moving away.

"Wait!" Alexandra called to her. "Zack and I will accompany you to the tavern."

Polly turned her eyes toward Alexandra, but kept walk-
ing. "Please, don't trouble yourself. It's only a short walk.
I'll be quite safe." Before Alexandra could protest again,
Polly crossed the street, hurrying toward the Blue Ram.

There was nothing for Alexandra to do but go home to
write a short report for the constable regarding the autopsy
on the stranger. She finished it quickly, detailing the blow
to the head and the apparent haste of the butchery that
followed. She would take the report to Snow later, after
she had finished her morning house calls and her surgery
hours.

In Nancy's absence, surgery hours did not go as
smoothly as usual, but it was important that she stay with
the Hastings baby. Alexandra was not surprised to see two
more cases of whooping cough, but she was thankful that
the patients were older children, who stood a much better
chance of survival than did little Alice. After she had seen
the last patient for the day, there was no more time left
to take her autopsy report to Constable Snow. She had to
relieve Nancy at the Hastingses.

Since she was accustomed to an early supper, she took
a small portion of the roast leg of lamb, which she had
removed from the oven earlier as Nancy had instructed.
The tender, moist texture of the meat and the delicate hint
of herbs surprised her, and she found herself taking a second helping. Artie and Rob, her two stable boys whom
she often invited to eat with her, were less pleased with
the delicacy, however.

" 'Tain't Nancy's cooking," Rob said, wrinkling his
nose at the pink slice of lamb in his plate. It was rimmed
with a rich and succulent brown edge.

"Look at it!" Artie said, pointing to an almost identical
slice on his own plate. "Why, 'tisn't even cooked. Ye can

see the blood in it, ye can. Needs a good boilin' like Nancy gives it, I say."

"You're absolutely correct," Alexandra said, touching her napkin to her mouth. "It doesn't taste at all like Nancy's cooking. Doesn't even taste English, I would say."

"Bloody shame, 'tis, too," Artie said, prompting a quick bop on the head from Rob.

"Watch yer language around the doctor," Rob said. At fifteen, he was the older of the two boys. Artie was no more than ten. He gave Rob an angry look and seemed about to start a row.

"I shall tell Nancy how much the two of you missed her culinary skills," Alexandra said before anything could develop further between the two. She put her napkin aside and stood. "You can take some of this bread," she said, pushing what was left of the loaf toward them. "Perhaps it will sustain you until Nancy returns."

"Yer goin' to relieve her soon, ain't ye, Doc?" Rob said, pushing his own chair back with such eagerness it tipped over when he stood. "I can 'ave Lucy saddled for ye in 'alf a second if yer ready to go."

"And I'll 'elp, too." Artie sounded equally eager.

"Your enthusiasm is admirable, boys, but I won't be needing Lucy for the short walk to Earl's Row." Alexandra spoke as she covered what remained of the leg of lamb with a cloth to return it to the larder.

"Ye'll take the beast with ye, will ye not?" Rob said. "There's danger about, ye know. What with people getting their hearts cut out."

"I'll take Zack with me for the walk to the Hastingses," Alexandra said, emerging from the larder. "But I'll send him back with Nancy. I shall be spending the night watching over the baby, and it will be bright morning daylight when I return, so there'll be no need of Zack's services."

"I think 'tis best we goes with ye. For protection, don't you know." Artie's statement might have been amusing, since he was a slightly built ten-year-old, except that the expression in his eyes was one of concern and fear far too heavy for one of his age.

"The chap's right," Rob said. "Zack's not enough. We'll walk ye over and walk back with Nance, then we'll come for ye on the morrow. Ye won't be walkin' the roads alone these days."

Alexandra started to protest but hesitated. Along with the genuine concern in the voices and faces of the boys, she had developed her own uneasiness about the senseless, random murders. "And what of your own safety," she said at length. "Who will be watching out for the two of you as you walk the roads?"

"We'll have ol' Zack, now won't we? Not a thing to worry about, miss," Rob said.

Alexandra thought of pointing out the inconsistent logic, but she had no time. She had to hurry upstairs to freshen herself before she went to relieve Nancy. The boys were waiting for her when she came downstairs with Zack sauntering along behind her.

" 'Tis a good thing ye got us to look after ye, I says." Artie's voice was bumpy as wadded cotton, because his short legs had forced him into a trot in order to keep up with everyone else.

When they arrived at the Hastingses, Nancy was busy reinserting the tube in the throat of little Alice. She had shown Kate how to hold the baby wrapped and tight against her body and shown Jack how to hold her head. Alexandra, who saw her through the open doorway, didn't interfere and waited until the task was done before she entered the house.

"The babe has been able to suckle twice," Nancy said as soon as she saw Alexandra, "but the night air has brought on the cough and the swelling again and robbed her of her breath. I thought it best to reinsert the tube, but we can't keep doing this."

Alexandra nodded. She and Nancy both knew the tube could irritate the passageway if they continued to remove and reinsert it. "Perhaps if we can get through this one night, we'll see improvement tomorrow. Have you used any of the red clover infusion?"

Nancy told her that she had administered it regularly and gave her a full report of the color, amount, and frequency of the baby's urine. "Did you have your dinner?"

"I did, indeed. I've never tasted lamb as succulent. I must remember to compliment Polly."

Nancy's reply was a long stretch of silence as she changed the baby one last time. Finally, she spoke. "I see you brought the boys with you." She glanced at Rob and Artie, who waited just outside the door.

"Yes, and we're 'ere to see you gets home safe," Rob called to her through the open door before Alexandra could respond. "We wouldn't want any danger comin' to *you*."

"Is that so?" Nancy's hands were on her hips as she gave the boys a suspicious frown. "And what mischief is it you've been into now that you think you have to get on the good side of me, pretending so much interest in my well-being?"

Rob stepped closer to the open door and shook his head slowly. "Ah, Nance, ain't you the suspicious one. 'Tis nothing but yer safety we're thinkin' of, and there's no mischief we've been at."

"It's best ye go with the boys, Nancy," Kate said, coming out of her fear and worry enough to speak for the first time. "There's that madman what walks about, ye know."

Nancy's hard suspicious expression weakened a little
as she was reminded of the truth, and she glanced quickly
in Alexandra's direction.

"I'll send Zack with you as well," Alexandra said, trying to sound reassuring. "Run along now, all of you, before darkness sets in."

"Have ye 'ad yer supper yet, Nancy?" Artie asked as
Nancy moved toward the door. "If ye've not et yet, it may
be ye could find a bit o' boiled mutton in yer kitchen, and
me and Rob could keep ye company whilst ye eats."

Nancy, stepping out the door, gave a little cynical
laugh. "Boiled mutton, is it? I should have known there
was a motive for your good deeds. And why would I be
serving you mutton now, anyway? There was the roasted
shank Polly cooked for all of us."

Alexandra could hear the boys' eager flattery as they
exclaimed their hunger and extolled Nancy's cooking
skills, their voices growing fainter as they moved away.
She turned her attention to little Alice and her parents.
Alice was restless, trying to pull at the tube in her mouth,
and the parents were still worried and hovering. When the
baby finally fell asleep from exhaustion, Alexandra was
able to persuade the parents to go to bed as well. Another
paroxysm of coughing awakened the baby in a little while,
and Alexandra was forced to remove the tube once more.
She tried the infusion of clover again, but it did little
good. If Alice had been at least two years old, she could
have given her belladonna. The narcotic would have
helped relax the reflexes that caused the cough, but she
dared not risk the dangerous side effects in one so young.
The baby's condition was extremely serious because of
her young age. Alexandra would not allow herself to think
about how slim the baby's chances of survival were. As

the night wore on, she found that the most she could do was hold the baby against her shoulder and either walk with her or rock her, humming a low, soothing, tuneless melody. The monotonous sound and the repeated movement seemed to mesmerize the baby so that she slept a little longer between paroxysms. She vomited after a particularly long period of coughing, and Alexandra had to awaken Kate to put her to breast in order to replenish the baby's strength. She would take very little of her mother's milk, however, and Alexandra soon had her back in her own arms again, pacing in front of an open window, since it was widely accepted that fresh air was an important element in the cure for whooping cough.

As she paced, Alexandra felt the darkness of the night seeping into her soul, staining her thoughts with its blackness until she felt trapped in a web of gloom. It robbed her of hope, so that she could think of nothing except Alice's slim chance of survival and of her own impotency in effecting a cure. She lacked the skills to overcome the laws of nature. She had exhibited that lack all too recently when she witnessed the death of the apothecary, Harry Neill, and his brother Winslow, who had come to her with ailments that defied everything she tried. Besides the troublesome rash, Winslow had developed respiratory difficulties as well.

Could that have possibly been whooping cough? After all, it did sometimes appear in adults, even in the aged. But she knew it could not be. The symptoms were wrong. The whoop at the intake of breath was absent. Their cases had been much more like severe influenza and inflammation of the lungs. Pneumonia, perhaps. But why had her attempts to cure them been so ineffectual?

Alice coughed again, so hard that the blood gushed from her nose and from her eyes, and Alexandra's mood

darkened even more. The appearance of the blood could
mean that Alice's brain was bleeding as well and most
likely swollen—a condition that could damage her brain.
Alexandra was helpless in her worry. There was nothing
to do but to walk her, to try to soothe her with a monotone
song, to try a few more drops of the clover infusion.

It was while she was in the depths of her personal darkness of despair that Alexandra glanced out the open window and saw a lone figure emerge from one of the
cottages on the opposite side of the street. She was certain
it was the same person she and Polly had seen disappear-
ing between buildings earlier in the day during the riot.
Polly had identified that person as Clyde Wright. He wore
the same cheap suit and equally cheap bowler set on his
head at the same jaunty angle, but she could not be certain
for herself that he was Clyde, since she hadn't gotten a
good look at his face.

Alexandra continued to watch as the figure crossed the
street diagonally. She could see that he carried something
in his right hand. It appeared to be a dirty white bag.
Alexandra leaned out the window a little to see him better,
still holding Alice against her shoulder. As he passed
through the light spilling from the window of the Methodist chapel, Alexandra leaned even farther out the window to try to get the illuminated view. Just as she did,
Alice, sensing the change in Alexandra's position, began
to cry, a hoarse sound that dissolved into another cruel
cough.

The sound alarmed the man. He glanced over his shoulder just as Alexandra pulled herself back from the window. Then he ran down the street, headed toward the
center of town, clutching the oddly stained bag to his
chest.

6

Alexandra left the Hastingses' house shortly before seven the next morning. She had been up most of the night trying to soothe and comfort little Alice and to do what she could to control her cough. Although the baby slept very little during the night, by six she had fallen asleep from exhaustion. Alexandra once again removed the tube, knowing that the baby would be hungry and eager to suckle when she awoke.

Jim had slept soundly all through the night, and Kate had been able to get at least a little sleep and, Alexandra hoped, would be able to care for Alice during the day. Alexandra planned to forgo her house calls and sleep a few hours before she opened her surgery.

She had no appetite for breakfast, since she was far too exhausted to think of anything other than rest, but Nancy, it seemed, had other plans for her. She had prepared a meat pie, along with boiled eggs and toast. Nancy appeared to be in a rather odd mood as she buzzed about

the kitchen, and Alexandra quickly decided it was best
that she not argue with her and, instead, at least try to eat
a little breakfast.

"Just some tea and a bit of toast will do, Nancy."

"Lost your appetite, have you?" Nancy's tone was
clipped as she removed the teakettle from the stove. "I
suppose that happens when one feasts on something as
fancy as roast leg of lamb. Succulent, I believe you called
it. Perhaps you meant overly rich?"

"Feast? I shouldn't think one small slice of lamb would
be called a feast. My loss of appetite is more a result of
losing sleep." Alexandra's weariness was evident in her
voice.

"One small *succulent* slice, wasn't it?" Nancy repeated
as she poured steaming tea into a cup she had placed in
front of Alexandra.

Realization came slowly to Alexandra as she raised her
eyes to Nancy's flushed face and her pursed lips. "Why,
Nancy, you *are* jealous of Miss Cobbe. Her culinary skills
as well as her abilities as an assistant in the surgery."

"Jealous? I should say not! I don't know where you get
such a notion." Nancy set the teakettle back on the stove
with a little too much force.

"Good. I'm certainly glad to hear you're not jealous,"
Alexandra said as she stirred cream into her tea. "Nevertheless, whatever name you choose to give your reaction, I assume I must reconsider your suggestion that I
hire her."

Nancy, busy filling the toast rack, spoke over her shoulder. "Perhaps I was wrong in suggesting it in the first
place."

Alexandra looked at Nancy over the rim of her cup.
"She does seem to have the proper experience, though,
doesn't she?"

"Experience?" Nancy turned to the table and put the toast rack on it with the same force she'd used placing the teakettle on the stove. A slice of toast tumbled out of the rack and onto the table along with a generous dusting of crumbs. She then sat down across from Alexandra and cut herself a large slice of the meat pie. "She got that experience caring for her sister and eavesdropping in the apothecary shop. Must I remind you again, 'tis not the same as being properly schooled by a competent physician such as your father."

"No need to remind me at all," Alexandra said, suppressing a smile.

"Not to mention the training I received the time the Florence Nightingale School conducted that short course for nurses at the hospital in Bradfordshire."

"Indeed."

"I certainly can't imagine why you would think I could possibly be jealous of mere experience."

"Perhaps I was wrong."

There was a long silence as Alexandra munched with disinterest on half a slice of toast and Nancy attacked her meat pie with what seemed to be a misplaced vigor. Nancy was the first to break the silence. "She's not Church of England, you know."

"Polly, you mean? Or Miss Nightingale?"

"Polly."

"Am I to assume not being a member of the Church of England represents a recommendation for her or against her?"

Nancy glared at her in response.

"Miss Nightingale, whom you admire a great deal, is a Unitarian, I believe, so perhaps it is a recommendation."

Nancy's glare faltered and she went back to attacking her pie. Alexandra decided she'd had enough sport at

Nancy's expense and spoke to her in a tone she hoped was reassuring. "Of course I won't hire Miss Cobbe, if you think it's unnecessary. You've always proved yourself to be quite efficient and capable of providing any assistance I need."

There was another long silence except for the sound of cutlery against china until Nancy, at last, put aside her knife and fork, cleared her throat, and spoke. "She is stuck in that dreadful charwoman position at the tavern, however."

Alexandra gave her a wry look. She'd always found Nancy's seesaw form of logic dizzying.

"And there are times, of course, when I *could* use a bit of help."

Alexandra set her cup down and pretended to be absorbed in brushing crumbs from her lap.

"Remember? I mentioned that."

"Yes, I believe you did. You said something about the patient load becoming heavier and the fact that you thought I might enjoy a bit of French cuisine now and then, which I believe you said Polly learned when she was a maid-of-all-work in France."

Nancy picked up her knife and fork and tried to resume interest in her breakfast. "I suppose you think I don't know what you're doing," she said.

"I beg your pardon?"

"Playing me like a violin, you are."

Alexandra felt a moment of chagrin. "Nancy, I—"

"Don't forget I'm the one who taught you such tricks."

Alexandra sighed. "I learned from the master," she said. "I suppose I forgot for a moment who the master is."

Nancy laughed with abandon, the kind of laugh that had been carefully and regrettably bred out of Alexandra. But Nancy's laughter was ruthlessly contagious, and Alexandra felt herself smiling, then having to cover her mouth with her napkin, until the contagion finally erupted from her in soul-cleansing bubbles of mirth. Within seconds, however, her laughter had evolved into sobs. She covered her face with her hands and wept until her shoulders shook.

"Miss Alex . . ." Nancy sounded shocked. She had rarely seen Alexandra cry.

Alexandra, embarrassed, did her best to control herself. "Forgive me, Nancy. I . . . I don't know what's come over me." She sniffed and dried her eyes with the backs of her hands then straightened her shoulders to regain some of her dignity.

" 'Tis all right, miss," Nancy said, reaching to cover Alexandra's hand with her own. "You're just a bit tired, now aren't you? Not yourself, I'd say. And who could blame you?" she added, giving her hand a squeeze before she stood and went to the stove to fetch the teakettle. "Up all night with the Hastings baby, and it doesn't look good for her, now does it? That's a worry for you, I know. And then all those murders and poor Gweneth being blamed." She poured Alexandra another cup of tea then poured one for herself. "Why, a weaker person would have been driven to pure insanity, I say." She sat at her place at the table again. "You'll be yourself once things return to normal."

Alexandra tried to smile and picked up her cup, grateful for the comfort of the familiar taste. She was embarrassed at her show of emotion, and she knew Nancy was right. Her lack of sleep had left her nerves frayed. "Will things ever return to normal, Nancy? All that's going on in Newton is pure madness."

Nancy nodded her head, but said nothing.

"It *is* madness, Nancy. The townspeople are right about

that. Only an absolute madman would do the kind of thing
we're seeing. Yes, they're right about that, even if they
have chosen the wrong people to blame."

"We're all on edge, Miss Alex. But try not to worry so
much. There is nothing you can do about it."

"Perhaps you're right." Alexandra suddenly felt overwhelmed with weariness. "But there should be," she
added in a voice so drained it was barely audible.

Nancy leaned closer. "Should be, you say? Now why
would you want to be taking on such a burden? Didn't
your father always warn you of trying to make yourself
God because of your talents and training?" Her voice was
scolding.

"If madness is a physical illness . . ." Alexandra spoke
more to herself than Nancy, and her eyes were focused
on something in another sphere.

Nancy pulled back from her. "Now don't be getting
into that old argument with yourself," she said. " 'Tis nonsense!" She stood and busied herself with clearing the
table. "All those doctors in London and America insisting
that madness can be cured with the right medicine if only
science could provide it! Why 'tis madness itself to think
that way. Insanity is not like a carbuncle that can be cured
with a poultice of poppy seeds. 'Tis in the mind, where
only God can go. Not in the brain, which man can manipulate with a bit of belladonna. Besides, we don't even
know who is committing all these murders, so how could
you cure him even if such a thing were possible? Now
you go on up to your room and sleep. You'll forget such
nonsense, you'll see. You'll be yourself again with a bit
of rest."

"Nancy, you don't understand. I—"

"Now, now," Nancy said, grasping her shoulders and
helping her stand. "Not another word from you, miss, until you've had your rest. You want to be in good form for

your trip to London on Saturday, don't you? Yes, of
course you do. Now up the stairs and into bed you go.
Zack, be a good dog and see that she stays there."

Alexandra couldn't summon the energy to protest
against Nancy's bossy manner. Neither could she manage
to form the words to ask why she was going to London
on Saturday, because Nancy kept up her patronizing chat-
ter all the way up the stairs and all the while she was
helping her change into her nightgown. By the time she'd
left, Alexandra could do nothing except fall into bed and
be grateful that she could no longer hear her impertinent
assistant.

She fell asleep quickly, but within four hours she was
awake. It was her habit to allow herself only a few hours
of sleep in the morning after she'd been up all night with
a patient, so she could more readily return to a normal
sleep pattern. She was up in time for the light lunch Nancy
had prepared, and she ate hurriedly so she would be finished in time to open her surgery for regular hours. Nancy
had been right—a bit of rest had done wonders for her.
Her body had lost its weight of weariness, and her mind
had cleared.

"You're looking much better, miss," Nancy said when
she saw Alexandra. "Ready for a good day's work, are
you?"

"Quite so, Nancy."

"You know, miss, I've been thinking," Nancy said as
she cleared the table. "It may be I *was* a bit peevish when
I saw how efficient Polly is at everything."

Alexandra glanced at her with surprise. Nancy was not
one to readily admit her shortcomings.

"I just can't stop thinking of her working as a charwoman in the tavern," Nancy said as if to explain her
unusual behavior. "And anyway, truth is she could possibly be a great help to me while you're in London. She

can tend to the kitchen while I take care of patients. Perhaps we could look at that period of time you're in London as an opportunity to determine whether a permanent part-time arrangement will be satisfactory for her as well as for me. For you, I mean." Nancy continued with her kitchen work and spoke with her back to Alexandra.

"I hadn't thought of it, but perhaps a probationary period would be in order," Alexandra said, realizing how hard Nancy was working at being fair. "I've decided against going to London, but that doesn't mean I can't hire Polly for a trial period." Alexandra had remembered she'd plan to attend a lecture on infection and the germ theory of disease, a subject in which she was particularly interested, but it would have to wait for another opportunity. She felt her presence was needed in Newton-Upon-Sea.

"Not going to London?" Nancy turned around to look at Alexandra, letting a pot she had just cleaned clatter to the floor in the process. "But you've been looking forward to this trip for weeks! You simply can't miss the opportunity to attend Dr. Lister's lecture on germs."

Alexandra shook her head, not allowing herself to think of the disappointment of missing what was likely to be a once-in-a-lifetime opportunity. "I can't leave you here alone, Nancy. Not when there is a mad killer loose."

"Nonsense, I—"

"The entire village is frightened," Alexandra said. "You can't belittle the danger."

Nancy stood in front of her frowning and with her hands on her hips. "Begging your pardon, miss, but do you really think your being here will make a difference in my safety? And," she added quickly before Alexandra could respond or defend herself, "Zack will be here. A good bark from that beast would scare away Satan himself."

"You can't be certain of that, Nancy."

"Then do you mind telling me exactly how you will protect me?"

"Well, I . . . It's just that I . . ."

"Anyway," Nancy said, " 'tisn't women who are in danger. If you'll notice, 'tis only men of a certain age the madman's after."

"There's no point in arguing with me. I've made up my mind."

"No time to discuss it now, miss. You must open your surgery," Nancy said.

In spite of her characteristic impudence, she was correct. It was time. In fact, the first patient was already knocking at the door, and Zack gave forth with a belated bark. Nancy turned away to pick up the pan she had dropped, and Alexandra hurried to the surgery. When she opened the door, she was both surprised and a little unnerved to see that it was Clyde Wright standing in front of her. His eyes were swollen and bloodshot as if he hadn't slept, and he was still clutching the dirty bag she'd seen him carrying during the night. When he thrust it toward her, she noticed the putrid smell and could see that the stains she had seen in the moonlight now, in the light of day, looked like dried blood.

"Clyde?" she said, doing her best to keep her voice from shaking. "I must say I'm surprised to see you. All of Newton thought you'd left town."

"Yes," he said, still holding the dirty bag toward her. "I left, but I came back." He thrust the bag even closer to her. "I want you to take a look at this."

"What is it?" she asked, holding her breath while she leaned toward him to peer inside the bag. In the same moment that she recognized the contents, Clyde spoke.

"It's someone's heart."

Alexandra found she could not speak.

"Maybe that stranger's."

"Good lord, Clyde. Why didn't you go to the constable when you found this?" Alexandra still stood in the doorway. She had not invited him to enter the surgery.

"What? That bastard Snow? Begging your pardon, miss, but I don't trust the man." He managed somehow to slip around her to get inside the surgery.

"This is clearly a criminal matter. Something Constable Snow should handle, and there's no reason for you not to trust him."

"Let's just say, I have my reasons, I do. And being a medical man myself, I know 'twould be of value to examine the tissue." Clyde once again thrust the bag at her.

Alexandra hesitated for the slightest moment and couldn't stop herself from peering inside the bag again. There was no questioning the fact that she was eager to examine the organ, but duty and common sense had to prevail. "I shall examine the specimen only after the proper legal procedures have been followed. You will come with me to the constable's office."

"You'll take it yourself, then." Clyde laid his package on her examination table and started for the door.

"No!" Alexandra spoke with such force that he stopped and turned around to look at her, an expression of what might have been alarm on his face. "You will go with me. The constable will want to know, as do I, how you came upon this." She picked up the bag and, before Clyde could take another step, moved between him and the door. She called for Zack and then for Nancy.

Zack, as was his custom, had been waiting just outside the doorway that led to the rest of the house. He pushed the door open with his nose and lumbered in, his eyes and ears alert, his enormous black-and-white body imposing itself on the scene with an authority that seemed to alarm Clyde even more.

Nancy arrived a few moments later. "Yes, miss?" she

said, then stopped suddenly, wrinkling her nose at the smell emanating from the package and staring at the visitor. "It's you, Clyde. You've come back, I see."

"And why wouldn't I come back?" He sounded defiant, but his voice was also laced with wariness. "There's a need here for an apothecary, is there not? And have I not proved my ability? Just ask any of old man Neill's customers. I'll do the whole town a favor and take over his shop."

"I see," Nancy said with her own brand of wariness. She glanced from Clyde to Alexandra. "Is there something I can help you . . . God in heaven! What is that smell?"

"It's a human heart, Nancy." Alexandra was not doing a particularly good job of keeping her voice calm. She had to push Zack aside, who was, by now, sniffing at the bag and growling nervously.

Nancy's eyes widened, and in spite of the alarmed and comprehending look in her eyes, she didn't seem capable of uttering a word.

"Clyde found this, it seems, and thinks I should examine it, but as I'm sure you will understand, I think the two of us should accompany him to the constable's office first." Alexandra was still standing between Clyde and the door as she spoke, and she was well aware of his nervous attempts to get around her. She had the sense that he would flee if he could. Her original plan had been to alert Nancy she was leaving and ask her to take care of any patients who arrived. Clyde's demeanor had changed her mind, however. She had decided she would need both Nancy and Zack to accompany them to the constable's office to help ensure that Clyde would not flee.

"Of course," Nancy said. Her quick mind had assessed the situation readily. "We must leave right away. Without our bonnets."

7

The gaol and the attached office of the constable were located in a section of town where ancient buildings lined a street named Griffon. These buildings had, over the centuries, begun to tilt from the top, forming a broken arch over the street like old women bending toward each other to whisper. Opposite the gaol was the pub known as the Blue Ram, where the assizes met when the judges were in town and where town meetings were held. It was a drab brown wooden building crisscrossed with shallow moldings.

Clyde, his face flushed, turned a longing glance toward the pub, which seemed now to be loitering in the afternoon sun. Clyde breathed a sigh as he, Nancy, and Alexandra approached the gaol. He had been animated with what Alexandra took to be nervousness during the entire walk from her house. His manner gave him more the appearance of a fidgety adolescent than a man in his mid-twenties.

"I fail to see the necessity for this," he said, holding back a little as they approached the door. " 'T'would simplify matters altogether if you would just examine the bloody thing and give the results to old Snow."

"Dr. Gladstone has told you the necessity." Nancy's tone was impatient. "Constable Snow will want to question you."

"Well, he can bloody well question me all he wants, but I got nothing to say except I found the damned thing."

"You would do well to mind your language when ladies are present," Nancy said, stepping in front of Alexandra to open the door to the constable's office. "And why are you so skittish about this? One would think you have something to hide."

Clyde seemed about to reply to Nancy's goading, but by then she had the door open and Snow was glancing up from his desk with a frown that could have meant either surprise or annoyance. Gweneth Pendennis, appearing tired and worried, stood across from his desk. Her son, Lucas, stood next to her, his expression confused. As soon as Nancy and Alexandra entered the room, his look of confusion gave way to a beaming smile of recognition.

"Look, Mama! It's Nancy. Did you bring me a sweet, Nancy?"

"Hush, Lukey," Gweneth said. She placed one of her arms around him and pulled him close, an awkward gesture, since he was both taller and heavier than she. They each placed a hand over nose and mouth in reaction to the smell of the bundle Clyde had brought.

"Be seated, please. I'll only be a moment," Snow said to Alexandra and her party. If he was curious about their presence, he showed no sign of it. Neither did he react to the smell of the rotting specimen. Instead, he simply turned back to Gweneth and addressed her. "You and your son may leave, Miss Pendennis. There are no charges against you."

Gweneth shook her head. "Please, sir. You were kind enough to rescue me from that mob and give me and my boy a safe night. Will you throw me out among the wolves now?"

Snow frowned at her. "I've kept you as long as I can. I have no authority to keep you longer, and even if I did, it is not a fit place for a woman and a boy."

"But, sir, I—"

"I shall keep a watchful eye on your house, miss. You must alert me of anything untoward, and now I must bid you good day." Snow turned his attention toward Alexandra. "How may I help you, Dr. Gladstone?"

Gweneth stood with her arm still placed protectively around her son for a brief moment longer before she turned away, as resigned as her position in life had taught her to be, but as frightened as her good sense demanded.

On the way out the door, Lucas stopped to look at Clyde and the bloodstained bundle he carried. "So 'twas you that buried it! It stinks! Why'd you dig it up?" He glanced at Snow. "If he gets to keep it, can I have mine back?"

"Lucas, wait!" Alexandra called to him. "What did you mean about Clyde burying . . ." Before she could say more, Gweneth picked up Lucas's hand and gave him a hard, quick jerk, pulling him out the door. Alexandra glanced at Clyde. "What did he mean about you burying something and digging it up again?"

Clyde shrugged, looking more annoyed than ever. "How should I know what he means. He's an idjet."

"What is this?" Snow demanded. He stood up from his desk and looked at the bag.

When it was obvious that Clyde would not respond,

Alexandra told Snow the story Clyde had told her. "I knew you had to be notified, of course. Before any examination is done."

"Quite so," Snow said. He had opened the bag enough to give the decaying organ a cursory glance, then pushed it aside. "I suggest you place that outside, Mr. Wright, and then I shall want to question you."

Clyde did as he was told and returned to stand once again in front of the constable's desk.

Snow instructed him to sit down, then, towering over him, he said, "Tell me exactly where you found that."

"In the woods, sir," Clyde said.

"Precisely where in the woods?" Snow glowered at him.

"At the edge of the village, sir. Opposite end from the sea. Near the road to Bradfordshire."

"Near Seth Blackburn's pigsties?"

"I wouldn't be knowing who Seth Blackburn is or where his pigpens is, sir."

"What were you doing in the woods?"

There was no response from Clyde. He kept his eyes glued on a spot at his feet.

Snow took a step closer. "I said, Mr. Wright, what were you doing in the woods?"

It seemed for a moment that Clyde would still not reply, but after a few seconds he spoke. "Nature's call, sir."

Alexandra was aware of the quick, embarrassed glance Snow threw in her direction, but she ignored it. She found it tiresome that anyone would expect either she or Nancy to be embarrassed by human bodily functions, given the circumstances of their professions.

Snow cleared his throat, showing a sign of his own rare

discomfort. "It was my understanding that you had left Newton-Upon-Sea."

"For a while, I did, but I couldn't find a decent position." Clyde's voice shook as he spoke. "When I come back thinkin' to ask for my old position, I heard about old Harry and his brother dyin', and I thought to stay on awhile and open up the shop on my own."

"You're not to leave town again until I tell you," Snow said.

Clyde came up from his seat a little. "But I had nothin' to do with none o' this, and I never took the money." He sank back into the chair.

Snow was silent, studying his face. "What money?"

"Why the money that's missin' from old Harry's . . ." Clyde's face went suddenly white.

"Money was missing from the apothecary?"

Clyde didn't answer. He must have realized too late that Harry Neill must never have gotten around to reporting the theft. Perspiration beaded on his forehead and in the hollows of his thin cheeks. Snow's protracted silence made him sweat even more.

Finally Snow spoke. "You took money from the apothecary?"

Clyde didn't answer, but his lips had begun to tremble.

"Did someone see you take the money? Ben Milligan, perhaps? That stranger found dead in the alley?"

Clyde suddenly came to life. "No! No, of course not. I told you I didn't have anything to do with none o' this."

Another long silence during which Clyde's face changed from white to gray, and Alexandra feared he would faint.

Snow broke the silence with another question. "Did you dig up the organ, as Lucas suggested?"

Clyde again answered quickly. "I did not! 'Twas just

laying there, I swear. Splattered it a bit with my own piss before I realized it."

"When did you find it, Mr. Wright?"

" 'Twas late yesterday. If the idjet was around, I can see why he thought I was diggin' when I went down on my knees to pick it up."

Lucas could not have seen him yesterday, Alexandra realized, because Lucas was in gaol. The boy must have seen someone else earlier.

"I find it odd that you should happen to stumble upon the organ at the edge of the forest when several of the townsmen and I spent more than a few hours scouring the area earlier searching for it." Snow's voice remained stern and intimidating.

Alexandra saw the knuckles of Clyde's hands grow white, but his voice was calm. "Yes, sir."

Before the words were out of his mouth, the front door flew open and everyone's attention, including Snow's, was turned to Seth Blackburn as he entered. Without acknowledging the presence of anyone else in the room, he stomped to the constable's desk, spewing anger and spittle. " 'Tis past the time ye puts an end to this, Constable! They's a pagan devil out there doin' this, they is, and if I spots 'er first, I'll splatter 'er blood from here to Spennymoor!"

Snow turned to him. "Calm yourself, Blackburn!"

Seth's lips were pursed, ready to spew more anger, but he quieted at the sound of Snow's voice and shuffled his feet uneasily.

"Now, you may state your business, but in a calm voice, and you must make it brief," Snow said, sitting at his desk.

" 'Tis me pigs, sir." Seth's voice trembled.

"What of your pigs?"

"They's dyin'! Them what ain't dead is sick. Staggers about, they does, like they's gone mad, then they's blood in their shit. Could only be the work of a devil what puts a spell on 'em. And I spied 'er on the street just now. 'Er with 'er idjet son. I never had this problem 'til they come to Newton. And now you sprung 'em loose again! They's full o' spite for me, they is, and I never done naught to them. They's out to ruin me, I say, and yer—"

"It is entirely possible that your swine have contracted a disease without the help of any evil spirit, Blackburn. I suggest you have a veterinarian examine one of the carcasses." Snow reached for a tablet on his desk and wrote something on it. "There is a veterinarian in Colchester, a Mr. Samuel McBride," he said as he wrote. "I shall send a telegram advising him of your situation, and—"

"And how will I be payin' a veternery?' Seth's face was red again. "Devils has wiped me clean of me livelihood, I tells ye!"

Snow put down his pen and studied Seth's face for a moment. "I shall contact him, nevertheless. There may be something he can do before other herds meet the same fate."

"And what bloody good will that be to me?" Seth asked, his anger boiling again. "We's overrun with lunatics and idjets and other evildoers. Ye'd best spend yer time stoppin' it, I say!"

"I shall do my best to end the evil." Snow stood and forced the paper into Seth's hands then took his arm and led him to the door. "In the meantime, burn the carcasses of your dead swine and separate the healthy from the sick."

"They's precious little of the healthy left, and the sows is birthin' freakish piglets. If ye don't do something, I'll have to take it into me own 'ands to—"

"Let me see your hands," Alexandra said, stepping between Seth and the door.

Seth gave her a startled, puzzled look. "What—"

"Your hands, please!"

Seth, still wearing his puzzled expression, held his hands out to her. Alexandra inspected them without touching them, instructing him to turn them over in order for her to see the palms as well. "You cover your hands with gloves when you tend the swine?" she asked.

Seth nodded affirmatively, bewildered.

"See that you continue to do so," she said. "Especially when you handle the diseased animals."

Seth's expression changed to alarm. "So's I don't touch the evil? Will it get me, too? Like the swine?"

"You'll be fine, Seth. If you do as I say," Alexandra said. "And see that you cover your mouth and nose with a kerchief so you don't breathe in dust from the pens."

The constable ushered him out the door and closed it, but Alexandra could still hear his muted and worried voice as he walked away. Alexandra caught Snow's eye as he returned to his desk.

"Anthrax," she said.

"A strong possibility, I'm afraid," Snow said.

"Oh dear God," Nancy brought her hand up to cover her mouth.

Clyde merely stared at everyone else with an expression on his face that was hard to read. It could have been either fear or bewilderment.

"If it isn't stopped, it can spread to all the farms," Alexandra said. "And to the farmers as well, and . . ." Her words trailed off as she thought of the lesions she'd found on the arms of Harry and Winslow Neill and Ben Milligan and the ones she'd seen on Kerwin Millsap's corpse.

"There could be an epidemic," Nancy said, finishing

her thought for her. "And it could spread to humans."

"Caustic potash," Clyde said. "And then a poultice of iodide of potassium, iodide of cadmium, glycerin, and powdered iodine." His glance slid from person to person. "I'm an apothecary, you know."

"We can try to treat the lesions if we get to them soon enough, but there isn't a good way to stop the spread among animals, is there?" Alexandra's concern was growing.

"There is some study under way on the continent," Snow said. "I read of it in a recent scientific journal. A chemistry professor by the name of Pasteur, it seems, has claimed to have found a vaccine of some sort. I trust McBride will know about it."

It was not surprising that Snow, a former schoolmaster, subscribed to scientific journals. Alexandra's interest was piqued. "Pasteur, you say? The same Pasteur who has studied fermentation and putrification of wine and milk?"

"I can't be sure," Snow said.

"It has to be one and the same," Alexandra said. "It's all part of his belief in the germ theory of disease."

"If it's a vaccine, then that means he's not likely to cure the ones who are already sick," Nancy said. "He can only prevent other animals from contracting it." She glanced at Alexandra. "Do you suppose the Neill brothers or Ben Milligan could have come in contact with Seth's pigs?"

Alexandra was not surprised that Nancy had come to the same conclusion she had concerning the men's mysterious disease, but judging by the troubled expression on her face, she was no closer to understanding the connection. "I suppose it's possible," Alexandra said.

"Perhaps you will find a clue to help solve that mystery

when you examine the organ Mr. Wright found," Snow said.

Clyde had been kept busy turning his head from one speaker to another, and he now spoke, addressing his words to Alexandra. "I told you, didn't I? Told you I brought it to you to examine. We could have saved a great deal of time had you not insisted—"

"Dr. Gladstone was correct in having you bring your find here." Snow's interruption was brusque, and as soon as he had spoken, he turned back to Alexandra. "You will do the examination?"

"Of course," Alexandra said. "Since I won't be going to London, I shall have plenty of time, although I must remind you, I found nothing helpful when I examined the first heart."

"London? You had planned a trip to London?" Snow appeared uncommonly interested.

"She was going to hear Dr. Lister's lecture on germs," Nancy said before Alexandra could reply. "And she should go. Hasn't gotten away in months. A trip would do her good, not to mention Dr. Lister's lectures would be invaluable to her. But she says she can't leave, what with all the dreadful murders and such."

"Nancy, please. Now is not the time to—"

"I agree with Nancy." Snow's comment caught Alexandra by surprise. "Of course you should go."

"But—"

"Perhaps you could be of more help in London than you would be here," Snow said.

"I don't understand. . . ."

"There is someone in London I would like you to consult while you are there." Snow's eyes had grown bright, a rare hint of enthusiasm. "A certain Dr. Kingsley Mortimer."

"A physician?" Alexandra asked, wondering if the constable had some illness he'd not told her about.

"An alienist."

"I see." Alexandra's expression belied the astonishment she felt. "You would like for me to consult with Dr. Mortimer regarding . . ."

"The recent murders, of course. You have heard of the criminally insane, I assume." Snow spoke with his schoolmaster voice.

"Bloody hell!" Clyde's eyes were wide.

Snow turned toward him with an expression that suggested he had forgotten he was there. "You may be excused, Mr. Wright. Since I've had no report of stolen money, and since Lucas was in gaol when the organ you brought in was discarded, he was obviously referring to someone else he saw burying it. There is no reason for me to keep you here."

Clyde rose to his feet and hurried out of the office without a word. The constable then turned his angry gaze on Nancy. "And you, Miss Galbreath . . ." He paused, frowning at her. "May keep your seat. But do keep quiet, please."

"Of course, sir," Nancy said with a sweet smile that made Alexandra suspicious. "I'm always rather quiet, you know."

The frown on the constable's brow became even deeper as he eyed Nancy, and he seemed about to speak, perhaps to refute her, but he turned his attention back to Alexandra as he resumed his seat. "I suspect, as I'm certain you do, that the heart is the one torn from the most recent victim."

Alexandra nodded.

"And I presume you agree, Lucas could not have seen anyone burying that particular heart, since he was in gaol at the time of the murder."

"Of course."

"I suspect the gossipmongers are right. It's the work of a madman."

"Certainly," Alexandra said.

Snow was silent a moment and seemed to be studying his hands, which were folded in front of him. "Dr. Mortimer has authored some interesting articles on the criminally insane," he said at last. He opened a desk drawer and pulled out a pamphlet, which he handed to Alexandra. "I suggest you read this one."

Alexandra glanced at the title, *Mental Science and Criminal Lunacy.*

"It's not the usual drivel about insanity being the result of an immoral life. At least not in the usual sense," Snow said. "He takes a rather interesting approach to lunacy, as you will see. Somewhat unorthodox medical view. That's why I think it is important that a medical person should be the one who speaks with him. I should like you to read this, and then discuss with him the matter of the two recent murders here. Perhaps he can help us gain insight into precisely the sort of person who might do such a thing."

"I shall be happy to read this, of course," Alexandra said, "but I'm afraid leaving Newton-Upon-Sea now is out of the question. My patients are—"

"Nancy is quite capable of attending your patients until you return." Snow seemed to make a point of not looking at Nancy. "It is precisely because she is versed in medicine and because she is your assistant that I allowed her to stay while I discussed this with you."

"Am I to understand, sir, that your conviction is that whoever is committing these insane acts is doing so as the result of a physical illness?" Alexandra asked.

"I have no convictions at all on the matter, Dr. Gladstone," Snow said in his usual cold voice. "That is the reason I wish you to interview Dr. Mortimer—to gain insight. I trust you will keep an equally open mind."

"But—"

"The constable is right," Nancy said. "You must go. And I shall be fine with your patients. 'Tis not the first time you left me the duties when you've found it necessary to be gone, you know."

"But if the whooping cough spreads, as I fear it will—"

"Then I shall take care of it." Nancy's voice was firm. "And remember, we agreed to ask Polly to help for a short time."

"Excellent," Snow said to Nancy and turned his gaze to Alexandra. "I should like you to leave as soon as possible. Perhaps tomorrow morning? I shall arrange for a carriage to take you to Bradfordshire. You can take the train from there." His tone of voice left no doubt that they were dismissed.

"I say 'tis a good thing you're going," Nancy said as they both stepped out of the office to retrieve the bundle before they began the walk home. "As for me, though, I'd be wary of a man who thinks insanity is a medical problem." She seemed about to expound further on her Cartesian view of the separate realms of the human body and the soul, but something distracted her. Alexandra noticed that her eyes were focused on a small gap between buildings just ahead of them. When she followed her gaze, she saw Clyde once again lurking in the shadows.

"What's he doing there?" Alexandra asked.

Just as she spoke, Clyde emerged from the shadows and gave both of them a look and a grin that could only be described as lascivious.

"That man gives me the jimjams," Nancy said.

8

Nancy carefully folded a freshly starched petticoat and placed it in the trunk next to the day dress of cream-colored linen with a matching hip-length jacket, which Miss Alex had chosen to take with her. The mistress had always insisted that Nancy construct her clothing in the simplest of styles. She especially eschewed the long trains that were the current fashion. Nancy had complied with her wishes and cut the skirt with only a short train and a bit of draping in the front. The only ruffles on the costume were at the ends of the tight-fitting, elbow-length sleeves.

While Alexandra's back was turned to search through a stack of her medical notes, Nancy took the opportunity to place another frock into the trunk. This one was made of light green faille with a neckline cut a bit low in the front as well as the back. The edges of the neckline were trimmed with ecru lace. While Nancy had kept the train relatively short, she'd pulled the overskirt back to reveal a silk lining and a pleated underskirt of the same color as

the lace. Alexandra had never seen the frock, and Nancy
was certain she would protest her packing it now, so she
quickly placed it beneath the plain linen dress. Miss Alex
would say the dress was impractical for her trip, and she
would insist on alternating between the cream linen and
her equally simply made brown traveling suit of summer
weight wool while she was there. But, Nancy thought,
there was always the possibility that her mistress would
want to indulge herself in a social event, and then
wouldn't she be grateful Nancy had thought to pack the
green faille?

Perhaps the possibility wasn't enormous, but there was
at least hope, wasn't there? Nancy had taken the liberty
of sending a telegram to Nicholas Forsythe, remembering
how Alexandra had met him at Montmarsh. Oh yes, those
were the days, Nancy thought. The days when the earl
brought his reckless, wealthy, and highborn friends to his
country house each summer for dinners and balls and
hunting parties. Miss Alex was sometimes invited to those
parties, and why not? Wasn't she equally as beautiful and
charming as any of the ladies? And while she might be a
few generations removed from the title, one of her ances-
tors had been a duke.

The problem, however, was that Alexandra had never
enjoyed the earl's friends or his parties, much to Nancy's
disappointment. Now, however, given the events of two
summers past, Nancy had to admit, however grudgingly,
that perhaps her mistress's reluctance had not been without reason. That was the summer the earl had been murdered by one of his own guests and his own wickedness
had been revealed as a result. The lovely house that was
Montmarsh had remained closed ever since. Nevertheless,
that was the summer Alexandra had met Mr. Forsythe, a
London barrister and the younger son of a viscount. In

spite of the fact that he dressed like a dandy and could be naïve about certain things in that odd way the highborn were, he had proven to have a head on his shoulders, and he seemed to have taken a liking to Miss Alex. Nancy suspected that Alexandra was equally fond of him. Nancy always enjoyed playing matchmaker, but she understood her mistress's reluctance to encourage Mr. Forsythe. There were certain events in her mistress's past. . . . Well, she wouldn't think about that now. Suffice it to say, Miss Alex was a challenge when it came to matchmaking, and Nancy always welcomed a challenge. So she'd notified Mr. Forsythe of the time and station of Alexandra's arrival in London.

"I went early this morning to check on the Hastings baby." Alexandra spoke over her shoulder to Nancy as she continued to write the report on the previous evening's fruitless examination of the heart Clyde had found. "I think there is small improvement, but her cough lingers still."

"More bleeding from her nose and eyes?" Nancy asked as she placed a lace-trimmed fan in the trunk, then took it out again. Alexandra hated fans. She placed a parasol in the trunk instead, in the hope that her mistress would at least acquiesce to that if the sun was sufficiently bright. She'd leave the umbrella out for her to carry in case of rain.

"Her mother told me of one more episode," Alexandra said.

"I don't have to tell you, 'tis the nature of the disease to run rampant in a town."

"Yes." Alexandra picked up her papers and tapped the ends on the small table to even them before she turned to face Nancy. "I only hope we're able to stem it somewhat."

Nancy was aware that two more cases had been re-

ported besides Alice and the Blackburn boy. At least they
were older children who stood a better chance of recovery
than the Hastings baby. "I have plenty of red clover infusion if 'tis needed," she said.

"Good. Yes, yes, of course. I know they'll be in good
hands." Alexandra sounded uncommonly edgy. But who
could blame her? Besides the precarious condition of little
Alice Hastings, there were those dreadful, uncivilized
murders. And now, the threat of anthrax in the area. All
the more reason to give her the opportunity to get things
off her mind for a bit.

"And Polly will be here, of course." Nancy had to keep
telling herself she would refuse to be jealous of Polly
Cobbe's skills. After all, it *had* been her idea for Miss
Alex to hire her in the first place. And it certainly was
true that she could always use a helping hand. It was just
that she hadn't expected Polly's skills to be so . . . well,
exemplary.

"I shall leave the decision regarding Polly up to you.
You know I trust your skills without question," Alexandra
said as if she'd read her thoughts.

That was when Nancy knew she was being foolish. Of
course there was no need for jealously. Her own skills,
she was confident, were equal to Polly's, and besides that,
there was a bond between herself and Miss Alex that no
one else had. "Perhaps I should invite her to stay here
while you're gone," she said.

"Oh, I didn't want to suggest that for fear you would
object, but I'm so glad you brought it up," Alexandra said.
"I know Zack will be here and Rob and Artie, of course,
and I know it sounds illogical, but I will feel ever so much
better knowing there's another person in the house."

"She's good company. I'm sure we shall both enjoy it,"
Nancy said and meant it.

Alexandra still had a worried expression on her face. "I just hope there'll be no more—"

"Don't invite trouble, Miss Alex. There's always trouble enough without an invitation. And anyway, the two of us will be fine here. Your mission for now is in London." Nancy hoped her choice of the word "mission" would have the proper effect on Miss Alex. She didn't want her backing out now on an all too rare opportunity to get away for a few days.

"Now who's playing whom like a violin? Don't you think I know why you're so eager for me to go to London?" Alexandra, with her hands planted on her hips, gave her an accusing look.

"Well, of course I'm eager. I know you're looking forward to hearing Dr. Lister—"

"London is a large city, you know. I don't expect to see Mr. Forsythe at all. He won't even know I'm there."

"Mr. who?"

"You are insufferable, Nancy."

Nancy, with her back turned, pretended to be busy smoothing out the already smooth and carefully folded petticoat that was packed in the trunk, but she couldn't keep a little smile from flicking across her mouth. Everything was going to work out wonderfully. She had told Mr. Forsythe in the telegram she'd sent that he was to give Miss Alex the impression that he happened only by chance to be at the train station when she arrived. It had cost her a pretty penny to send the message because she found she couldn't keep her words from multiplying. There was so much she needed to tell Mr. Forsythe, and she couldn't possibly get it all in one message.

"And don't try to pretend now that you're not as concerned about these awful murders as I am. You see danger lurking in every corner," Alexandra said.

Nancy turned and glanced at her, eager to defend herself. "Of course I don't. Why would you say—"

"What was that you said about Clyde Wright? That he gives you the jamjims?"

"Jimjams," Nancy said, correcting her. "But that doesn't mean I'm frightened."

"What does it mean?"

"Well," Nancy said, beginning to feel trapped. "It simply means that he . . . That I . . ."

"He gives me the jamjims, too. He has a rather . . . well, unpleasant air about him, doesn't he?"

"Now that you mention it . . ." Nancy was reluctant to delve too deeply into the unpleasantness of Clyde Wright at the moment, but the truth was, she had been wondering about him recently. It seemed a bit odd that he had disappeared for a time and then reappeared just as the two gruesome murders had taken place. Of course it could have been mere coincidence, yet . . .

"Nancy! Are you listening?"

"What? Oh, yes, of course, miss," she lied.

"Then tell me."

"Tell you what, miss?"

"What was preoccupying your thoughts so? Something about Clyde Wright?"

Nancy hesitated for a moment, trying to decide what to say. She was tempted to deny that she'd been thinking of Clyde, but it seldom worked to lie to Miss Alex. She was far too clever. "It's just that . . ."

"Yes?" Alexandra urged her.

"Well, it does seem a bit odd, doesn't it, that he disappeared for a while and—"

"And then suddenly reappeared when the murders took place," Alexandra said, completing her thought for her. "Yes, I've thought of that myself." She shook her head.

"But that could be a coincidence, and the fact that he's rather repugnant doesn't justify our suspicions."

" 'Tis always been my belief that a woman should pay attention to her instincts. Even when it seems improper to do so. 'Tis the gift of second sight, you know, a woman's instinct. One must cultivate it."

"Good lord, Nancy, you can be utterly pagan at times."

"Call it pagan if you like, miss, but we both know, without knowing why, that there's something about that man that makes us uncomfortable. And besides, he has always wanted that apothecary shop for his own."

Alexandra frowned. "And how does that relate to anything?"

"Well," Nancy said, wondering why Miss Alex couldn't see the logic, "it seems obvious that he couldn't have it unless Harry Neill was dead, and his brother Winston as well, since he would be his only heir. With both of them out of the way, he could grab the shop for very little—"

"Excuse me, Nancy," Alexandra interrupted, "but you're making no sense at all. Harry and Winston Neill died of blood poisoning, possibly as a result of anthrax, but . . ." She stopped speaking and appeared to be thinking as a puzzled frown creased her brow.

"You're thinking what I'm thinking, I can tell," Nancy said.

"Of course I'm not!" Alexandra looked annoyed.

"Yes you are!"

"But it doesn't make sense, I tell you." Alexandra slammed the trunk lid shut.

"What doesn't make sense?" Nancy said as Alexandra was on her way out of the room. "That Clyde could have caused the two brothers to contract anthrax? Of course he could have."

Alexandra stopped and turned to look at her, the annoyed expression she'd worn now replaced by a troubled one. "Even if Clyde could have somehow caused the Neill brothers to contract anthrax, why would he have caused Ben Mulligan and Ferwin Millsap to contract it?"

"I don't know, but I would bet they were supposed to die of anthrax, and when they didn't, someone, Clyde, maybe, made sure they died another way."

"Why? What could possibly be his motive for them to die and for the stranger to die?"

Nancy shrugged. "They saw him stealing money from the shop, as the constable suggested? I don't know. I'm not saying I have all the answers, miss. I'm just saying I have a feeling about that man. And if it doesn't make sense now, 'tis only because we haven't opened our eyes to our own second sight."

Miss Alex looked at her without speaking for a long moment, but it was impossible to tell whether or not she was considering what Nancy had just said. Finally, she spoke. "Where could he . . . where could anyone get the anthrax strain with which to infect others?"

Nancy shook her head slowly. "I don't know, miss. Perhaps . . ."

"Perhaps we should stop such foolish speculation," Alexandra said.

"I was going to say, perhaps we should keep using that second sight."

Alexandra gave her an annoyed look and left the room without speaking. Nancy had seen something in her eyes, though, something that let her know her mistress would not discard everything she'd said.

*   *   *

*It was early the next morning when Constable Snow ar-*rived with his carriage to drive Alexandra to the train station in Bradfordshire. Alexandra had left Nancy with instructions she knew were unnecessary. She was more than capable of taking care of most of the needs of the patients who came to the surgery. Now that some of the more progressive hospitals were seeing the value of medically trained nurses, Nancy could, no doubt, find a lucrative and satisfying career in a large London hospital. Alexandra had offered her that opportunity, but Nancy refused, saying she could think of nothing more satisfying than the position she held. The words that would express the sense of sisterhood and the dread of separation they both felt had remained unspoken between them.

Alexandra was still uneasy about leaving in the wake of the recent murders in Newton, but she did her best to convince herself that Nancy and Zack as well as Rob and Artie would be safe.

The ride to Bradfordshire was uneventful, and since Constable Snow was seated in front, driving the carriage, while Alexandra was seated behind him, their conversation was limited, and Alexandra found herself dozing. As a result, she was surprised at how quickly they seemed to arrive at the train station. The constable bade her a hasty farewell and gave her a letter of introduction to Dr. Mortimer along with his address in London.

It was late by the time the train reached London, and a slow, steady rain fell from a dark, grumbling sky. Alexandra's brown traveling suit was rumpled, and her heavy auburn hair was trying, with some success, to free itself of the restraints of its pins. She had removed her hat for comfort's sake within a few minutes after she boarded the train, and she was only partially successful at taming her hair enough to force it under the hat before she disembarked. Her concern was not with her hair, however, but with the task of hiring a hansom to take her to the small, inexpensive, but respectable hotel where she always stayed on her infrequent trips to London.

She lifted her gaze above the sea of umbrellas that protected the individuals waiting outside the station from thin silver threads of rain and focused on the doorway leading into the station, sighting her goal and hoping to make her way there quickly. She felt a moment of shock when she recognized the man who seemed to be loitering in the doorway. Nicholas Forsythe, dressed in a grey frock coat and a matching high-crowned hat. In spite of the fact that he had grown a mustache since the last time she'd seen him, there was no doubt in her mind that it was he. Neither was there any doubt that he had seen her and, for some reason, promptly stepped back away from the doorway and out of sight. Rather odd, she thought. Why would he not want her to see him? Perhaps he had come to the station to meet someone—a woman perhaps, and he wished to avoid an embarrassing moment if he had to introduce her. Well, he need not be embarrassed, she thought. After all, there was nothing between the two of them other than a casual friendship.

As she stepped off the train and onto the platform, she shifted the small black medical bag she always carried, in order to raise her own umbrella, and made her way through the crowd to the equally crowded station. Its high-arched nave and transepts gave it the effect of a sanctuary devoted to the worship of chaos. The first thing to do was to see about hiring a hansom and porter to help with her trunk once it was unloaded. She was mentally calculating the cost when Mr. Forsythe appeared suddenly in front of her.

"Dr. Gladstone!" His eyes were wide in pretended surprise as he removed his hat. "What a pleasant surprise to find you here. I've just put a colleague of mine on the train to Oxford and was about to leave. Pray tell me what brings you to London?" His speech sounded, oddly, as if it had been rehearsed.

"Good evening, Mr. Forsythe. It is indeed a surprise." She tried to sound properly congenial, but she couldn't keep her eyes from shifting toward the front of the station where the cabs waited. If she didn't keep moving forward, she feared there would be none left to hire. "I've come to attend a medical lecture tomorrow, and I do hope you'll forgive me, but I must hurry before all of the cabs are gone."

"A cab? Nonsense. I shall be happy to take you in my carriage." He gave her a dazzling smile, and for the first time she noticed that his frock coat and matching hat were not really grey but a most luxurious hue of silver and that his hair had been trimmed to a very modern and fashionable shorter length. She had forgotten that he was actually quite good-looking.

"That's very kind of you, but I . . . I shall be happy to accept," she said, changing her mind as she realized how inconvenient it would be to continue to stand in the rain trying to secure a hansom. "If it's not too far out of your way, that is. I'm staying at the Wheatcroft."

"Not at all out of the way," Nicholas said. "It will be my pleasure." He took her arm and led her toward the exit and a carriage waiting a few yards from the entrance. Alexandra was barely settled in the seat when the darkening sky was cloven by a brilliant crackling flame. At the same time thunder, like an angry god, roared from somewhere above and a great crush of rain fell from the sky. Nicholas shouted his instructions to the driver and ducked inside, seating himself next to Alexandra while they waited for her trunk. His fine coat was mottled by the rain and his tall hat studded with wet diamonds.

"You're looking well, Dr. Gladstone, and if I may say so, quite lovely. I trust all is well in Newton-Upon-Sea?"

"Oh yes, quite so," she said, the lie slipping off her tongue with an ease that surprised her. It was simply that she was tired and didn't wish at the moment to go into the detail of all that was not well in Newton-Upon-Sea.

"Mmmm," Nicholas said and frowned. For a moment it seemed to her as if he knew she was not telling the truth, but that, of course, would be impossible.

"And Nancy? And Zeke?"

"Very well, thank you," she said, not bothering to tell him her Newfoundland was called Zack and not Zeke. He was only making small talk anyway, since he had never seemed particularly fond of Zack, and it was, under ordinary circumstances, highly unlikely that a gentleman of his class would ever inquire after the welfare of a servant. Undoubtedly the inane conversation was because he felt awkward having her in his carriage. If he did, it would be much better, she thought, to remain silent.

"I say," he said, continuing nevertheless, "I envy your opportunity to hear Dr. Lister's lecture on the germ theory. The idea of a whole world of tiny animals invisible to the naked eye causing disease and putrification fascinates me."

Alexandra turned to him and smiled in spite of herself. "It is fascinating, isn't it? The germ theory has been around for almost four decades, but there's so much we don't know. I should say it's rather like reading a new chapter in an exciting novel. Every time something new is discovered, I mean."

Nicholas returned her smile. "What is more fascinating is your interest in such matters."

"I beg your pardon?"

"You are a unique woman. I'm quite unaccustomed to the likes of you."

"A woman who is a medical doctor, you mean." She'd heard this before, often accompanied by hints of disapproval. Nicholas had never shown any signs of disapproval on the other limited number of occasions she'd been in his presence, however.

"Oh, it's more than that, although a member of your sex being a physician is rare enough. No, it is that you are, in some ways, more alive than any woman—or man, for that matter—I know."

"You flatter me, Mr. Forsythe. I am not yet permitted to use the title 'physician' since I was not allowed to complete all of the courses at university that would grant the title to me. I am merely 'surgeon.' "

"More's the pity," he said almost flippantly, then added, "Tell me, what do these minute animals—germs, I believe—what do they look like, precisely?"

"Rather like tiny rods, some of them," she said, unable to resist. The truth was, she was every bit as fascinated as he pretended to be, and she was always eager to discuss the germ theory of disease. The conversation continued after her trunk was loaded and during the long drive through the rain. After a while she became convinced that Nicholas's interest was genuine. He guided the conversation until it had advanced to the theory of vaccination and how it might be that germs are rendered impotent by it. She was interrupted in her explanation when the carriage stopped, and the driver shouted something that was impossible to hear over the sound of the relentless storm.

Nicholas slid the protective window curtain back and called to the driver. "What is it, Farley?"

Within seconds the driver was standing at the window

in his soggy livery shouting and gesturing. " 'Tis the street, sir. Flooded, she is. They's no way we can pass. No way to the 'otel. Broken sewer main, I'd wager."

Nicholas answered him without hesitation. "Then take us to Kensington." He turned to Alexandra. "You'll sleep under my roof tonight."

"Oh no, that won't be necessary, I'm certain . . ."

"Of course it's necessary. We can go no further in the direction of the hotel. Our choice is to stay here in the rain or drive to Kensington."

Alexandra hesitated a moment, reluctant to take his suggestion, but he was right, there seemed to be no other way. "Very well," she said finally, with resignation.

In the same instant, Nicholas said, "Please don't object and don't concern yourself with the appearance of impropriety. I can assure you that—"

"I accept your offer, Mr. Forsythe. I am rarely concerned about appearances. Rather I shall be grateful."

He seemed stunned for a moment. Then he smiled slightly before he spoke. "Excellent! I shall have a surprise for you in the morning."

9

The richly paneled walls of the entry to Nicholas's house were lined with family portraits, and a wide and graceful stairway led to the upper reaches of the house. The stone floor was partially covered with a dark burgundy Oriental rug woven in an intricate design. As Alexandra stood admiring the elegance, she was aware of an effortless beauty peculiar to those who were born to wealth. She was aware also of the man, she assumed he was a butler, who had opened the door and now stood waiting discretely for Nicholas to speak.

"Morgan, summon Broomsfield, please, and see that she has the blue room ready for Dr. Gladstone. And tell Cook we'll be needing a light supper."

"Right away, sir," Morgan said with a slight bow then disappeared through a door at the end of the hall. If he had been at all curious about her, Alexandra noted that he hadn't shown it in his unchanging expression.

Nicholas turned to Alexandra. "I assume you haven't eaten."

"No, but please, there's no need—"

"Perhaps you'd like to freshen up a bit first. Morgan!" The butler reappeared almost instantaneously. "Show Dr. Gladstone to her room, and see that her trunk is brought in." He turned to Alexandra again. "Will half an hour be enough time?"

"Really, it's quite unnecessary—"

"Good. Half an hour, then. I shall freshen up myself, and meet you in the dining room. Morgan will show you the way."

"If you would wait in the drawing room for just a moment, please, Doctor," Morgan said. He opened the door to a pleasant room where several gas lamps burned brightly and a small fire burned on the grate. As in many of the older houses in London, the night air made the room cool even in summer, especially on a damp night such as this one.

Alexandra settled herself in one of the chairs and had begun to doze when Morgan reappeared. He gave her another of his little bows and said, "Your room is being prepared, Doctor. I'll show you the way, if you please." He gestured with an open hand toward the stairs then followed her up the wide curving staircase to the landing, where a large window overlooked the back of the house. Perhaps there was a garden there, Alexandra thought, but the rain and darkness kept it from her.

Morgan directed her a few steps down the hall then stopped to open the door to one of the bedrooms. Inside a young woman of perhaps twenty, dressed in a black dress with a crisp white apron and cap, was smoothing a coverlet. She looked up, straightened her posture, and curtsied. Alexandra sensed Morgan surveying the room before he spoke again. "Broomsfield will see to your needs, Dr. Gladstone. And when you're ready, the dining room is the large room on the left downstairs, just past the library. He turned away and was gone before Alexandra could collect her thoughts.

As she stepped inside, her eyes were drawn immediately to a large painting hanging above the fireplace mantel and dominating the room. It depicted a young woman with delicate features wearing a filmy dress of soft blue, standing relaxed and graceful against a dark background. That appeared to be the only thing in the room that suggested it might warrant the name "blue" room, as Nicholas had called it.

Alexandra saw, too, that her trunk had already been brought up, presumably by the back stairs, and now rested at the foot of the brass bedstead. A tall wardrobe made of dark mahogany, a matching dressing table, and a washstand were the only other furnishings apart from a small cabinet next to the bed which would, of course, hold the chamber pot.

"Will you be wanting to freshen up a bit, miss?" the maid asked in a voice as thin as skim milk. "There's fresh warm water in the pitcher." She pointed to a porcelain pitcher sitting inside a matching bowl on the washstand.

"Thank you," Alexandra said, eager to take advantage of the opportunity to wash away some of the sweat and grime of her journey.

"And will you need help dressing your hair, miss?"

The question caught Alexandra off guard. Her hand rose unbidden to touch the unruly strands that had broken free of their pins. She was quite unaccustomed to having anyone help her with her hair—or any of her toilet, for that matter—and the thought of it annoyed her for a reason she didn't fully understand. "That won't be necessary," she managed to say.

"If there's nothing else, then . . ."

"What? Oh no, nothing, thank you."

The girl gave her a quick little bow and, mercifully, left the room. Alexandra breathed a sigh of relief and removed her hat and jacket. Her hair, free of only part of its pins, hung in uneven strands about her face and shoulders. The reflection of herself she saw in the mirror reminded her of an unkempt scrub woman. Nicholas, of course, had been too much the gentleman to have commented, but she had no doubt he had noticed. There was a moment of acute embarrassment, which she forced away quickly, angry with herself. It had been a long time since she had been concerned about her looks because of a man, and she told herself she was not about to resume that folly.

Yet she couldn't deny the pleasure of a cloth dampened in the warm water as she moved it slowly over her face, her arms, her neck, and beneath her chemise to her breasts; nor could she deny the delightfulness of the soft caress of the towel as she dried herself. Feeling more relaxed, she slipped the last of the pins from her hair, took a brush from her trunk, and pulled it with long, slow strokes through her hair, her eyes closed, allowing the ritual to relax her even more.

Her eyes flew open suddenly as she remembered Mr. Forsythe's comment. *I envy you your opportunity to hear Dr. Lister's lecture on the germ theory.* How could he have possibly known that was her reason for traveling to London? And in the same instant she knew. Nancy! Impertinent, meddling, conniving Nancy. And Mr. Forsythe, equally conniving. At the station to see a companion off, indeed!

She put the brush down on the dressing table with a

thud and gathered her mane of hair quickly in her hands, rolling and twisting it and pinning it into place with a speedy fierceness, then put her jacket on and buttoned it quickly. She was about to leave the room, but she couldn't resist one last glance in the mirror; and then, in spite of her resolve, she gave her cheeks a pinch to bring forth some color, and then walked brusquely out of the room and down the stairs to the dining room.

Nicholas waited at the door and smiled when she appeared. "May I say, you look remarkably refreshed and lovely, Dr. Gladstone."

"Nancy must have notified you somehow," she said, ignoring his compliment.

Nicholas's eyes widened and his smile disappeared. "I beg your pardon."

"It was not a chance meeting, was it? She told you the date and time of my arrival." By now she had reached the door and they stood face to face.

"Perhaps we should be seated," he said, holding the door open for her.

Alexandra studied his face a moment, noting the benign expression. His demeanor was so practiced, so like a clever barrister. Frustration lashed at her. "How could she have possibly gotten a message to you so quickly? I only decided late yesterday."

"This way, if you please," Nicholas said, guiding her with a hand on her elbow toward the long table, its polished surface a glimmering cherry-wood river reflecting light from a single candelabra at the end. The table was set with two places, one at the end and another next to it on the right, more intimate than cozy. Alexandra hesitated slightly, but Nicholas's firm but gentle grasp of her elbow was unrelenting. He led her to her chair and held it while she sat, then took his own place at the head of the table.

"She sent a telegram," he said before he was completely seated.

This time it was Alexandra's eyes that widened in surprise. Her expression was met by Nicholas's finely chiseled mask, betraying now a parenthesis of humor at the corners of his mouth.

"Nancy? Sent a telegram?"

"Quite the modern lass," Nicholas said, allowing his mask to crumble and fall into the depths of his smile. "And, I shall add before you do, cheeky as ever."

"Quite so!" Alexandra still sounded angry. Morgan appeared behind her, pouring wine into a glass.

"I'm sorry I betrayed her somehow. I did my best to make it look like a chance meeting." It was humor, not regret, that danced in his eyes. Brushing his mistake aside quickly, he said, "I know you eat a light dinner, so I took the liberty of ordering a simple meal."

He had scarcely finished speaking before plates of poached salmon and baked mullets were brought in and placed on the table by a servant. "Allow me," he said, placing a portion on her plate first, and then on his.

Alexandra stared at her plate, feeling disconcerted that he should remember such a small detail as her preference for a light dinner. She tried to push the feeling away as she picked up her fork and sampled the salmon. It was uncommonly delicious.

"Tell me," Nicholas said. "How did I give it away? The fact that I knew you were coming, I mean."

"You mentioned Dr. Lister. You could not possibly have known I planned to attend his lecture unless someone—Nancy, to be exact—had notified you."

"How careless of me."

Alexandra suddenly saw their situation as acutely embarrassing. She put down her fork and touched her napkin to her lips. "Allow me to apologize for Nancy's placing you in such an awkward position. I will most certainly speak to her and see that she doesn't do it again. And while you have been most gracious and generous, I'll not impose upon you further. I shall find a hansom and—"

"I'm afraid I rather doubt that," Nicholas said. "That you will see that Nancy does or doesn't do anything, I mean." He seemed to be laughing at her with his sea-colored eyes. "She's rather like an unruly pup, I say. But witty. I'll grant her that. Almost a match for you." He held her eyes with his for a moment and she saw something ancient burning in their depths. In spite of that, he went on with his banalities. "Leaving in this weather would be most unwise as well as ungenerous, as you would be depriving me of your company."

"Really, Mr. Forsythe—"

"What is it, Dr. Gladstone? What is it that makes you so cautious? You hide behind your caution."

He had once again caught her off guard, and for a moment she thought he might have, in his uncanny way, glimpsed that part of her she kept hidden even from herself, but she recovered quickly, at least to the extent that the wine, which was now making her dizzy, would allow. "Perhaps it is my profession," she said with as much aloofness as she could muster.

He spoke nothing, but his eyes said everything, or at least enough to make her feel uncomfortable. She was relieved that the moment was interrupted by the servant bringing in the next course. She took a small portion of the beef as well as of the larded sweetbreads but found that, in spite of their superb flavor, she could eat very little of either.

"Shall I call for another entrée?" Nicholas asked. "Perhaps a larded guinea-fowl would be more to your liking."

"No. Thank you. As you said, I'm accustomed to a light dinner." She had stepped behind her barrier again, and she knew he was aware of it as well.

"Whatever you wish," he said. She saw him raise his chin slightly, and in the next moment Morgan was pouring more wine for her. "Perhaps a dessert?" Nicholas said.

"No. Thank you, I've had quite enough. And I'm afraid I'm rather tired," she added. "If you don't mind, I should like to retire early." It was a lie, of course. She didn't feel at all tired now, after her short nap while she waited for Morgan, but she was afraid he would ask her to join him in the drawing room. That was something she would ordinarily have looked forward to. He had spent long hours in her parlor in Newton-Upon-Sea discussing a variety of subjects that she'd found intellectually stimulating, just as they had discussed the germ theory of disease on their way to his house. But something had changed between them, something she didn't understand. Perhaps it was being here in his house that made her feel so disconcerted. Or perhaps it was the rain pounding on the roof and the wine pounding in her veins and Nicholas seeing far more than she wished to reveal.

She was grateful that he didn't protest her early retirement and grateful to be alone in the confines of her room. The bed had been turned back, and the soft glow of a lamp next to her bed seemed to invite her in. It was altogether an immensely enticing scene, and she was eager to slip into bed and to push all thoughts of Nicholas from her mind—to fall asleep thinking of nothing except the anticipation of an enlightening and stimulating lecture tomorrow.

She was surprised by a soft knock on her door. "Yes," she called over her shoulder with some impatience.

" 'Tis me, miss. Broomsfield. I come to see if you need anything before you sleep."

"Thank you, no," Alexandra said, thinking how she missed Nancy, who knew her habits well enough not to interrupt when she didn't wish to be.

"Mr. Forsythe instructed me to open the window. He said you would prefer the fresh air even if 'tis night air. But the rain . . ."

"Thank you, it's quite all right," she said, and then, because she was once again taken aback by how much Nicholas seemed to know about her, added in defiance, "I shall open it myself when the rain stops."

When she had undressed and gotten into bed, she lay on her side, staring at the painting of the woman, barely visible by the dim light that still burned at her bedside. It was a trick of that pale light and the dancing shadows it threw out that made the woman's face appear animated, as if she were trying to tell her something. Something pleasant, Alexandra thought, as she allowed her thoughts to drift. She fell asleep thinking not of lectures on the germ theory of disease, nor of murder in Newton-Upon-Sea, but of Nicholas.

She awoke the next morning with the day already dressed in sunlight and birdsong. She was briefly disoriented, not knowing for certain where she was. Then, realizing the truth and the obvious late hour, she sat upright. As if on a cue, there was a knock on her door. It seemed to her now as if it had been only minutes since the last knock. Before she could respond, the door opened slightly, and Broomsfield peered around the edge. Alexandra instinctively pulled the coverlet up to her chin as the girl entered.

"Ah, you're, awake, miss. I brought your breakfast," she said as she entered, carrying a tray covered with a linen napkin. "I hope 'tis eggs and cold beef you like, along with muffins and a bit o' tea." She placed the tray across Alexandra's lap and removed the napkin. She waited patiently until Alexandra let go of the coverlet, then placed the napkin over her chest. "Will there be anything else?" the maid asked as she poured the tea.

"What time is it?" Alexandra asked, ignoring the tray.

"Half past nine, miss. Mr. Forsythe has gone to his office, but he said to tell you that you are to make yourself comfortable until he returns at half past eleven for the luncheon with you and the other guest."

"The other guest? Who?"

"I'm afraid I wouldn't be knowing that, miss." Broomsfield stood with her hands folded in front of her, waiting. It took Alexandra a moment to realize she was waiting to be dismissed.

"That will be all, Broomsfield," she said. Her tone, she realized, was a little too sharp, but it was her own behavior that disturbed her, not the maid's. She had planned to rise early and hire a cab to take her to the address Constable Snow had given her for the alienist. She would interview him, she had reasoned, and still have plenty of time to attend Dr. Lister's lecture at two o'clock in the afternoon. It must have been the wine that made her sleep the morning away. Now, she knew there was not enough time to carry out her plan. She would have to wait until tomorrow to meet with Dr. Mortimer. The best she could do now was see that no more time was wasted.

"Broomsfield!" she said, calling the maid back when she was barely out the door. At the same time, she moved the breakfast tray aside, jumped out of bed, and pulled on her dressing gown.

"Yes, miss."

"I must write a message," Alexandra said, buttoning the

dressing gown. "I shall need pen and paper as well as someone to deliver the message." She had decided to send a message to Dr. Mortimer informing him of her wish to see him, and she would instruct the messenger to wait for his reply.

"Yes, miss," the maid said again.

She was gone only a few minutes when a knock came at the door. When Alexandra opened it, she was surprised to see, not Broomsfield with pen and paper, but another servant, this one a girl of no more than fourteen, carrying two large pails of steaming water, one in each hand.

"Good morning, miss," the girl said. "Broomsfield said I was to help ye with yer bath whilst she sees to yer request."

Alexandra was astonished. "My bath? But I . . ."

The young girl entered the room and set the two pails of water down while she pulled a metal tub from the bottom of the wardrobe closet. Next, she took a bottle of liquid from her apron pocket, poured it into the tub, and then poured the steaming water over it. A delicate scent of lavender rose up with the steam. Alexandra continued to watch, speechless, as the girl brought the stool from the dressing table and placed it beside the tub then placed the towel from the washbasin rack on the stool, along with a bar of soap, which she took from another apron pocket.

She stepped back from the tub and asked, "Will you be needing help with yer buttons, miss?"

"With my . . . ? Oh! No, I shall be quite all right," Alexandra said, eager for the girl to leave. When she was gone, Alexandra stared at the tub and inhaled the lavender scent for a moment, then, deciding it was too inviting to resist, unbuttoned her dressing gown. She picked up the cup of tea Broomsfield had poured and set it on the stool before she slipped into the water.

She had enjoyed both her soak and her tea for several minutes when Broomsfield returned. "It's me, miss," she said from outside the door. "With yer writing paper."

Alexandra was nonplussed, silently chastising herself for having succumbed so quickly to such decadent behavior that allowed her not only to sleep until half past nine, but also to forget her duties as she lounged in a bath of scented water. "Just a moment," she called, scrambling out of the tub, drying quickly, and slipping into her dressing gown before she opened the door.

"Danny is waiting downstairs. He'll deliver the message, miss," Broomsfield said, standing by while Alexandra wrote the note requesting a meeting. "Shall I ask him to wait for a reply?"

Alexandra told her yes, then handed her the note. By the time she was dressed and downstairs, it was past ten. She still had more than an hour to wait for Nicholas to return for luncheon. It would be rude to leave, of course, but the wasting of time made her restless. Even a short stroll through the still damp gardens behind the house didn't consume enough time. She went back inside, hoping to find the library, where she could at least pass the time reading.

The library was not difficult to locate. A door was open just up the hall from the room she knew to be the dining room, and when she passed by, she saw that the walls were lined with leather-bound volumes. Stepping inside, she was momentarily surprised to see that she was not alone. A woman stood near one of the bookcases, wiping dust from the top of a row of books with a white cloth. She was a rather handsome woman of about sixty, small of stature. She was wearing a dark dress with delicate lace cuffs and an old-fashioned lace cap. She could have been mistaken for a highborn lady, but her dusting cloth gave her away.

"Forgive me, I hope I'm not disturbing your cleaning." Alexandra spoke in a quiet voice so as not to startle the housekeeper. "I just wanted to find something to read while I wait for Mr. Forsythe to return for luncheon. I shall be out of your way in a moment."

The woman turned to look at her with pale blue eyes framed by delicate lashes and finely arched brows. "It's quite all right, miss. And I shall be happy to have you remain here with your book if you wish. You shan't disturb my cleaning at all." Her accent and grammar were impeccable. How like Nicholas to have a housekeeper of such caliber. The woman made one more wipe at the books, then folded the cloth and placed it inside her cuff as if it were a handkerchief—a rather odd gesture, Alexandra thought. But having lived with Nancy practically all her life, she was accustomed to servants with odd habits.

"Thank you," Alexandra murmured, glancing at the shelves in front of her. They were packed with law books. She turned toward another shelf and happened to spot a book lying facedown on a nearby table as if someone, Nicholas most likely, had left it that way to mark his place. She picked it up and noted the title. *Ben Hur.* She had heard of the book. It was new and gaining in popularity, especially among the less intellectual. It was said to be a rather well-researched historical romance in a biblical setting and written by an American who was a territorial governor in an American province called New Mexico. Interesting that a man in an uncivilized wilderness should be so knowledgeable of ancient Roman and Jewish history, Alexandra thought as she scanned a few pages.

"Were you looking for anything in particular?" the housekeeper asked.

"No, nothing in particular," Alexandra said, replacing the book to the table. "I'm afraid I'm just a bit restless."

"Indeed?" The housekeeper's fine brows rose a bit.

"Please don't concern yourself," Alexandra said. "It's all my own doing. I'm afraid I made a terrible mistake by staying here, in spite of the storm. I'm afraid I'm simply going to waste Mr. Forsythe's time, and certainly my own."

"Come now, my dear," the housekeeper said in a half-scolding tone. "There's no point in grieving over anything you call a mistake. I believe that we may look back on any particular moment of the past and truly feel that it was impossible, God's laws being what they are, that we should have done other than as we did."

"Perhaps you're right," Alexandra said, a bit taken aback.

"Of course I'm right. Guilt is counterproductive and remorse is not a true feeling." She moved across the room until she was face to face with Alexandra. "Think of it this way. God himself is the author of all evil for which we blame ourselves, so that through our mistakes we will find truth."

"An interesting theory." Alexandra was genuinely intrigued. "And rather bold, I might add. There are those who believe God will punish you for daring to speak your mind that way."

"Oh, I believe in God's punishment all right," the housekeeper said.

Alexandra gave a little laugh, enjoying the lively conversation. "You seem to have contradicted yourself. You undoubtedly mean you believe in His mercy."

"Not at all!" The woman tossed her head as she spoke

until her cap was slightly askew. "God must inflict us with evil consequences for our sins and ignorance. Otherwise, how would we learn? Mercy would be cruel."

"I suppose you believe in eternal damnation, then." Alexandra prompted her, the way she might have done Nancy.

"Certainly not!" The housekeeper was indignant. "God administers only remedial punishment. How could eternal damnation promote human progress?"

Alexandra was about to ask her if she thought human progress was truly a divine purpose when she was startled by Nicholas's voice behind her.

"Dr. Gladstone! I see you've already met Miss Nightingale. She's the surprise I promised you."

10

Nicholas wanted desperately to speak to Alexandra in private, but he was momentarily distracted by the puzzling expression on her face. The sudden rush of color, however, was rather attractive. It gave her a fresh, girlish look. Then, the odd conversation that followed between her and Miss Nightingale puzzled and distracted him even more.

"Miss Nightingale, I must apologize. I didn't know—"

"Of course you didn't, Dr. Gladstone. And I didn't know you were a—"

"But there's no way you could have known since I—"

"Likewise there is no way you could have known that I am—"

"I'm afraid I was rude since I assumed you were the house—"

Miss Nightingale laughed. "I should have told you. I spied a smudge of ink on one of the volumes, and I can't bear to see a book defaced. It was rather amusing, really, that you—"

She laughed again, and oddly enough, Alexandra laughed as well. The two of them gave each other one of those pseudo-embraces that women are inclined to perform in which they almost but not quite cause the sides of their faces to touch. Then, as if they'd purposefully conspired to confuse Nicholas even more, they each turned to him as if they expected him to say something pertinent.

"Shall we . . . have lunch?" he said lamely and stepped back for the two of them to precede him to the dining room.

The two women exchanged a look, the meaning of which he had no inkling, and walked into the dining room. The formality of the room was relaxed somewhat by the intimate seating, with Nicholas at the head of the table and the two women on either side of him. When they were seated, each spoke to him in a most charming manner, thanking him for arranging the luncheon. He accepted with as much grace as he could muster. He was now regretting the fact that he had arranged the luncheon. Not that he didn't find each of the women charming in her distinctively different way. It was simply that he had heard some quite disturbing news about Newton-Upon-Sea while he had been in his office. He was having difficulty focusing on the conversation.

"But statistics, of course, give us insight into how those laws operate," Miss Nightingale said. Nicholas had no idea what she was talking about. Miss Nightingale, like Alexandra, however, did very much enjoy philosophical discussions, and she was a great proponent of the science of statistics. He had been introduced to Miss Nightingale by his mother, one of the few women who, as far as Nicholas could tell, called the outspoken and opinionated woman friend. For now, however, it was a struggle for

him to listen to what he ordinarily considered her enlightening if sometimes shocking opinions. He was much too
concerned about Alexandra. Perhaps it was unreasonable
to think she was in danger because of what he had learned
about the recent gory murders in Newton, but he was concerned, nevertheless. He was also puzzled that she hadn't
mentioned the deaths. She had always been an enigma to
him.

"And I'm sure you agree that the mischief in that is
obvious, don't you, Mr. Forsythe?" Alexandra said.

"What?" Nicholas felt momentarily disoriented. "Oh
yes, the mischief. Obvious. Yes, of course, you're quite
correct." All he could think of now was getting as much
information from Alexandra as possible. But she would
insist on attending that lecture. He'd have to think of
something. Perhaps he should keep her here indefinitely,
especially if there was danger in Newton-Upon-Sea.

"Is it too much to hope that before the millennium—
before the year two thousand—that no longer will be the
case?" Miss Nightingale said, addressing her question to
him.

Nicholas, by this time, was so bogged down with concern he could not think of even the simplest response. The
best he could muster was a blank stare.

"Mr. Forsythe, are you ill?" There was genuine concern
in Alexandra's voice.

"Ill?" he said, slowly coming out of his fog. "Of course
not, I'm . . ."

"You really should have told me the physician who
would be joining us was a woman, Nicholas," Miss Nightingale said as his voice trailed off. There was a lilt in her
tone, as if she might be teasing him.

"And you certainly should have told me to expect Miss
Nightingale," Alexandra added. "I'm afraid I made rather
a fool of myself in the library. But of course, it would be

ridiculous for me to blame that on you," she added with a charming laugh. "I seem to be able to manage that quite on my own."

The two women were obviously enjoying themselves. He had to be careful not to spoil it. There would be time after lunch to speak to Alexandra, and it would be best if he didn't betray his worry now.

"Nonsense!" Miss Nightingale said. "It is abundantly clear you're no fool, my dear. Please, you must tell me a little about your practice."

"There's nothing extraordinary about my work, Miss Nightingale. I'm a country doctor with a practice among people I've known all my life. A practice, I might add, that I inherited from my father, who was quite instrumental in my training."

"Dr. Gladstone is being far too modest." Nicholas was making a special effort not to appear distracted. "She's quite well respected in her community and displays a remarkable affinity for the practice of medicine. You would admire her efficiency."

"You're being too kind, Mr. Forsythe," Alexandra said. "You know Nancy is largely responsible for my efficiency."

"Nancy?" Miss Nightingale glanced first at Nicholas then at Alexandra.

"Dr. Gladstone's nurse," Nicholas said. "You will be pleased to know she's quite well trained."

"Excellent!" Miss Nightingale said.

"And how is Nancy?" Nicholas spoke up quickly before Miss Nightingale could launch into one of her discourses on the importance of trained nurses.

"Quite well, thank you. She would be pleased that you asked." There was an oddly strained quality to Alexandra's voice that hadn't been there before. Perhaps, Nicholas thought, she was worried about having left Nancy alone in Newton. "I am rather concerned about having left her," Alexandra said as if she'd read his mind. "We were on the threshold of a pertussis epidemic when I left."

"Pertussis?" he asked, feeling disoriented again.

"Whooping cough," Miss Nightingale said by way of explanation before Alexandra could respond. "Another infectious disease transmitted through the air, especially in overcrowded conditions. Perhaps one of those diseases Monsieur Pasteur would like to study with an eye toward inoculation."

"Interesting thought," Alexandra said. "Monsieur Pasteur has done some remarkable work with inoculations, but I suspect a whooping cough vaccine will be a long time coming. Pity you weren't able to meet him when you were in France."

"Indeed. I would have welcomed the opportunity. I find the theory behind inoculation interesting, but I would like to debate the value of it, compared to public education regarding sanitation, with Monsieur Pasteur."

"Will Nancy be able to handle it?" Nicholas asked, for no particular reason other than to appear interested. "The epidemic, I mean." He had realized too late that his question seemed to be out of context. Both women were looking at him with slightly bewildered expressions.

"For a while I believe," Alexandra said finally. "I shan't leave her for long, of course, and fortunately, she does have help."

"You've hired another nurse?" Nicholas was still only pretending interest.

"A woman we've met who seems quite capable as a result of having cared for her younger siblings. You may know her, Mr. Forsythe," Alexandra said. "She's been employed at the local pub for some time, and I know you've purchased lodging in the inn above the pub when you've visited Newton. Her name is Polly Cobbe."

"Cobbe? I'm afraid the name doesn't sound familiar." Nicholas was wishing profoundly that they could have dessert and the luncheon would end.

Miss Nightingale spoke again. "Polly Cobbe, you say? If it's the Polly Cobbe I know, her capability stems from considerably more than having cared for siblings. Is she by chance a rather pleasant-looking blond woman, plump of figure?"

"Precisely." Alexandra's tone reflected heightened interest.

"An excellent cook, by chance?"

"Indeed, you do know her!"

"I met her when I was last in Paris." Miss Nightingale waved away a servant's offer of dessert as she spoke. "I met with a group of nurses while I was there, and she was among them."

"A trained nurse?" Alexandra appeared surprised.

"Yes, she is from the working class, you know, and she'd been brought to France with a family who employed her as a servant. Then, when the family returned to England, she stayed in Paris and attended nursing school. Terribly bright girl. Became quite fluent in French. The language as well as the cuisine. I know, because she prepared a meal for a group of us."

"I'm sure you're relieved that Nancy has the competent help of an experienced nurse," Nicholas said. He was trying desperately to think of a way to end the conversation, in the hopes that Miss Nightingale would leave and he could ask Alexandra about the Newton murders.

"Miss Cobbe was not actually employed as a nurse when I met her, so I can't speak for her competence," Miss Nightingale said.

Alexandra gave her a puzzled look. "But didn't you just say she—"

Miss Nightingale raised a cautionary finger as she interrupted her. "I said she was with a group of nurses, and I said she was trained as a nurse. When I met her, she was on holiday from her job and was visiting with some of her former schoolmates who were nurses. The same nurses I happened to meet with. Miss Cobbe, however, had taken another direction. She had become a laboratory assistant to Monsieur Pasteur."

Alexandra set down a glass she was about to raise to her lips. "Really? Rather odd choice for her, I should think."

"Yes, I suppose it is odd," Miss Nightingale said, "but it shouldn't be. Women of all classes are denied the right to satisfy passion or intellect or moral activity. Perhaps we are partly to blame ourselves for this. But," she added with a wave of her hand, "to say more on this subject would be to enter into the whole history of society and the present state of civilization."

Nicholas felt momentarily relieved that she didn't seem inclined to begin that discussion at the moment. Yet, to his dismay, Alexandra seemed determined to carry on in a previous direction, as they all removed to the drawing room for coffee.

"I also find it odd that Polly never mentioned she was a laboratory assistant to Monsieur Pasteur," Alexandra said.

"Perhaps it is odd," Miss Nightingale agreed, "although I do seem to recall she wasn't inclined to be enormously talkative. Not about herself, at least. A trait which I admire, I might add. But then, perhaps being an assistant involved nothing more than cleaning the laboratory. Perhaps there was nothing about her position to warrant mentioning."

"Mmm," said Alexandra, considering it. "She did work as an assistant at our local apothecary, but one would think—"

"Now that I think of it, we did have a bit of a discussion regarding Monsieur Pasteur's work," Miss Nightingale interrupted. "Miss Cobbe was quite interested in his research. *Fascinated* perhaps would be a better word, although I can't say she led me to believe she understood a great deal."

"I wouldn't expect she would," Alexandra said.

"Of course not, and mind you neither do I have a deep understanding of the science and mechanics of disease. It is my contention that mankind should use statistical analysis to determine what sort of living conditions must be avoided in order to encourage a healthy society rather than concentrating on ridding the world of the organisms of disease. As I mentioned, that is what I should like to discuss with Pasteur."

"I must say, I don't agree with you entirely," Alexandra said.

"Few people do," Miss Nightingale said with a little laugh.

Nicholas was about to attempt to take advantage of the interlude created by that small laugh to say something that he hoped would bring the luncheon to a close, but he was preempted by Miss Nightingale.

"Nicholas, dear, you've been uncharacteristically quiet. Perhaps I've dominated the conversation too long. But I do find Dr. Gladstone most interesting." She extended a hand to him. "Please help an old woman to her feet, dear boy. I shall be going so as to allow Dr. Gladstone time to get to the lecture."

"You mustn't be in such a hurry. You know I'm always glad to have you dominate any conversation." In the same moment that he lied so easily, Nicholas stood and gave her his hand to help her out of the chair.

Miss Nightingale laughed again. "You are really quite

charming, Nicholas, even when you're not being entirely truthful. Please do give your mother my love." She turned to Alexandra. "It has indeed been a pleasure to converse with you. I am always happy to find one of my own kind who has been allowed to develop her mind." She offered her hand to Alexandra.

As soon as Miss Nightingale was gone, Alexandra turned to him and spoke. "That was a delightful luncheon, Mr. Forsythe. Miss Nightingale is truly an interesting person, I must say. And with such an analytical mind!"

"She is indeed," Nicholas said, "but let's not talk about Miss Nightingale or her analytical mind now. There's something I must discuss with you."

"There's nothing I'd like better than to talk with you, Mr. Forsythe, but you must forgive me. I haven't much time before I must leave for the lecture, and I really must see if I've received a reply to a message I sent by one of your servants." Alexandra seemed restless and kept glancing toward the back of the house where the servants would be.

"I hope you didn't send young Dan," Nicholas said with a chuckle.

"Why yes, Broomsfield suggested I use him. I hope there's nothing amiss."

"Oh no, nothing amiss," Nicholas said. "It's just that Danny has a tendency to dawdle. I hope you weren't expecting a quick return. He'll return eventually, but who knows when. He's quite easily distracted and a bit slow, I'm afraid."

A troubled frown creased her brow. "Certainly I'd hoped to hear before I left for the lecture this afternoon. I haven't long to stay in London, and I was seeking an appointment with someone at the request of Constable Snow."

"Ah yes, Constable Snow," Nicholas said. He had met the constable on two other occasions when he'd visited in Newton-Upon-Sea. "Does his inquiry by chance have something to do with the rash of rather brutal murders that have recently taken place in your charming village?"

Alexandra appeared stunned for a moment. "I had no idea news from such an out-of-the-way place as Newton-Upon-Sea would travel so quickly."

"It is the age of electricity and machines, Dr. Gladstone. I learned the unfortunate facts in a telephone conversation with a colleague."

"But we have no telephones in Newton." Alexandra sounded a bit confused.

"No, but the telegraph wires reach that far. My colleague received a wire message from a rather distraught pig farmer wanting to know if he could bring suit against a witch for killing his pigs. He asked the farmer for more details, of course, and learned of the murders in the farmer's reply. Seems the farmer thinks the murders are connected somehow to his dead pigs."

Alexandra's puzzled frown deepened.

"Oh, I know what you're thinking. You're thinking there was no good reason for my colleague to call me, but there is, of course. He knows I have a connection to Newton."

"You have a connection to Newton?" Her voice was full of doubt.

"Well, yes, as a matter of fact I do. You see I'm involved in the legal aspects of determining who is the rightful heir to Montmarsh. It's rather complicated, you know, since the late Lord Dunsford had neither progeny nor siblings, and there is more than one claim to his holdings."

"I should think that would be a task for a solicitor."
Alexandra appeared to be distracted and losing interest,
Nicholas thought, since she was once again glancing to-
ward the servants' quarters.

"Why did you not tell me about the murders?" he
asked.

She suddenly turned her attention back to him. "I've
hardly had time, Mr. Forsythe, and how could I have
known you'd be interested in the first place?"

"I am more than interested, Dr. Gladstone. I am concerned for your well-being."

"How . . . kind of you."

He thought he saw her cheeks color slightly, and he
expected her to look away, but she did not. He tried to
hang on to the moment. "You are so . . ." Words failed
him. Did he want to say she was beautiful? She was not
conventionally so. Her mouth was too wide and she was
too tall and perhaps a bit too thin. But her skin was the
color of ivory, and he had seen that beautiful auburn hair
once, quite by accident, when it was unbound and wild.
She wet her lips and looked away, and it was in that
moment that he decided her mouth was not at all too wide.
It was at once sensuous and intelligent. He wanted to tell
her so, but before he could form the words, she spoke to
him.

"There is no need for you to be concerned about me
since I am quite safe here in London. But as you can
imagine, I am concerned for Nancy and Polly as well as
my stable boys, and while it may be irrational for me to
think I could do anything to protect them, I am, nevertheless, quite anxious to return to them."

There it was again—that mask of propriety she wore.
It made him more determined than ever to learn why she
felt the need to protect herself from him. If he could keep

her in London and in his house long enough, he would find a way to get behind that mask. "Perhaps," he said, deciding not to push the matter too hard, "you could give me the name of the person you wish to contact on the constable's behalf, and I could hasten a response from him."

"There is simply not time." Her old edginess had returned. "I must leave within a few minutes for the lecture, and by the time I summon a hansom——"

"I shall use the telephone, but I must have the name of the party you wish to contact. I can even arrange a meeting. Oh, and no need to call a hansom. I've already arranged for my driver to take you in my carriage."

She stared at him without speaking for the span of two heartbeats. "If it's possible to contact the doctor, I would appreciate it. His name is Dr. Kingsley Mortimer, and while your second offer is generous, there is no need to have your driver——"

"I insist."

Another pause, and then, "Very well."

It took several minutes for central exchange to make the connection with Dr. Mortimer's office, and during the wait a new worry began to nibble at him. Why was Alexandra seeing a doctor in London? Was she ill? Was her claim that Constable Snow had requested it just a way to cover up the fact that she was not well? Was it just another aspect of the mask she wore?

It was not until a clerk answered the telephone on Dr. Mortimer's end with a stilted phrase—"Dr. Kingsley Mortimer, alienst and neurologist"—that Nicholas realized what Snow was thinking. The murders were the work of a madman. He turned the telephone over to her, and by the time she had arranged a meeting with Dr. Mortimer, he knew he had to find a way to accompany her.

11

❧❧❧

Dr. Joseph Lister's lecture on infection and the germ the-
ory of disease was delivered to an audience that practically overflowed the small lecture room at the university.
No talk regarding the theory of germs as the cause of
disease was possible without the mention of Louis Pasteur, however. It was that name that caused Alexandra's
thoughts to stray during the lecture, in spite of the fact
that she was truly interested in Dr. Lister's theories.

Miss Nightingale's revelation that Polly Cobbe had
once been an assistant in his laboratory still puzzled Alexandra. It wasn't that Polly was not capable of serving
as a laboratory assistant, and certainly her having trained
as a nurse might, in some way, be an advantage. The
puzzle was that Polly hadn't mentioned either her training
or her work for Monsieur Pasteur. The puzzle was com-
pounded by the fact that she hadn't taken advantage of
her training to find a position better than that of char-

woman. Perhaps she had something to hide. Could Nancy somehow be in danger?

Alexandra chided herself for such negative thoughts and returned her attention to Dr. Lister's lecture. He was demonstrating how disease-causing microbes react to certain chemicals. She was able to focus her attention for several minutes before her thoughts drifted back to Nancy and Polly and the recent disturbing events at home. There seemed to be no sane or sensible reason for all that had happened. If it was the work of a madman, she could only hope that Dr. Mortimer could provide some insight, as the constable suggested.

Dr. Mortimer hadn't seemed particularly eager to see Alexandra when she finally was able to speak to him on Nicholas's telephone device. Or perhaps it was the device itself that made it seem that way. She had felt awkward speaking into the mouth of the dark metal object while she held its appendage to her ear for listening. Dr. Mortimer's voice had a queer, distant, and somewhat tinny sound to it as it came to her ear from somewhere inside the appendage. To respond to him, she had felt the need to shout into the thing's mouth since he was on the opposite side of London. Nicholas whispered to her that there was no need to shout, and she had lowered her voice to a normal range, causing Dr. Mortimer to complain in a very unpleasant manner that he was unable to hear her.

The entire experience left her feeling drained and a bit disconcerted. It did seem, however, that she had secured an appointment to see him in the evening. Dr. Mortimer's entire demeanor had changed once she mentioned Constable Snow's name. He assured her that he would most certainly make time for her, and that yes, the constable had sent him a wire that someone would be calling on his behalf, and he was terribly sorry that he hadn't known she was the person who would call, but he would be very pleased to see her this very evening if she would come to his home near the asylum where he worked. He was quite eager to discuss what Constable Snow had revealed to him in the telegram, he said, and he even offered to send a carriage and driver for her.

Dr. Lister moved deeper into his discussion of the germ theory of disease and once again mentioned Monsieur Pasteur's work, this time regarding how the theory led to the development of vaccines for both humans and livestock. His latest work, according to Dr. Lister, involved a vaccine for anthrax in sheep. Alexandra had no idea how he had made the transition from antiseptic surgery to anthrax in sheep, and she was once again having trouble maintaining a focus on the distinguished physician's words until he brought his remarks back to diseases in human beings.

The act of forced concentration had been demanding and tiring for her, and she was relieved when the lecture ended, in spite of the fact that she knew it had undoubtedly provided new insight into the practice of medicine and to surgery in particular.

She walked out of the lecture hall expecting to look for a hansom since she had instructed Nicholas's driver not to wait. She was barely out the door when she heard her name called in a voice so deep and rich it seemed to be made of chocolate.

"Dr. Gladstone. Paging Dr. Gladstone."

She quickly found that the source of the voice was a giant of a man with the look of Scotland about him—fair hair that was wild, unruly, and almost red—and a face that life had carved into a craggy landscape. He was dressed in livery, as incongruous on him as an Eton jacket would have been.

It took her a moment to work her way through the crowd to his side. He was still calling her name and searching over the heads of everyone around her.

"I am Dr. Gladstone." His height made her feel like a child, as she had to look up to speak to him.

His pale eyes widened as he looked down at her. "You?"

"Yes. I am Dr. Alexandra Gladstone."

He continued to stare at her a moment longer, as if she were some odd specimen he'd never seen before, then his eye crinkled out a smile and a brief burst of strong, round laughter forced his head back. "You?" he said again, looking at her. "Doctor Mort did nae warn me 'twould be a woman," he added, tumbling every R around on his tongue a few times before he let it escape.

"Warned you?"

"Ah, you must pardon my bad manners, milady. 'Tis just that I was nae expectin' a lady is all."

"Am I to assume you were sent to fetch me by Dr. Kingsley Mortimer?" Alexandra couldn't help smiling. There was something about the man's pleasant face and manner that put her at ease.

The man nodded affirmatively. "Sent a carriage for you, he did. Said I was to find and deliver one Dr. Gladstone, so you can see why I naturally thunk 'twas a man I'd be afetchin'," he said.

The big coachman turned and, with his rich, round, and resonating voice, cleared a way through the crowd to the carriage. They were soon on their way through the streets of London. It was a long ride to the hospital on the opposite side of the city. The sun, self-satisfied with its day's work, had turned to a lazy bronze by the time they reached the long, stretched-out building that was the Beckwell Hospital for the Insane.

The brick structure, with two wings spreading from each end of the tall center, looked like children's blocks laid side by side, some jutting out farther than others, some stacked higher. It was set amid parklike grounds and gave the appearance of ultimate modernity. The carriage circled around one side of the building to a respectable middle-class house at the edge of the grounds.

When Alexandra knocked with her gloved hand on the door, it was opened by a tall, silver-plated woman who must have been in her fifties. She wore a grey dress with an apron of a darker shade of grey, and her grey hair was pulled severely from her face and wound into a bun at the back. Her thin face, which was neither pleasant nor unpleasant, looked as if it had never been marred by a smile. "This way, please, miss," she said before Alexandra had a chance to speak. She led her toward a room just off the hall, where a portly gentleman with a white-flecked beard sat relaxing in a chair, sipping a glass of brandy.

He put aside the brandy and rose to his feet as soon as he saw her. "You are Dr. Gladstone, of course. Please come in." He gestured toward a chair then turned to the silver woman. "Tea, please, Gerta." His voice was cordial but not particularly warm. When Alexandra settled herself in the chair he had indicated, he turned to her again and spoke in his same lukewarm voice. "It is a pleasure to meet you, Dr. Gladstone."

"Thank you," she said.

"Tell me, please. How is Robert?" He seated himself in the chair opposite her.

"Robert?"

"Snow. How is he?"

"Constable Snow. Of course. Quite well," she said, noticing for the first time that his eyes did not match his voice. Those eyes burned with something.

"Good," he said, nodding. "He's a good man. As you may know, I met him through his sister."

"Did you?" she said, hoping to cut short the polite banalities. There was nothing to say anyway, since she hadn't known until that moment that Constable Snow had a sister.

"Yes, well, but that's another story, of course." He cleared his throat and leaned toward her slightly. She got a faint whiff of the brandy as he spoke. "Robert sent me a wire and told me to expect you, but as we all know, one is not able to go into great detail with a telegram. He said only that the subject is a series of murders on which I might be able to shed some light and that you would explain the details."

"I shall do my best," she said, accepting the tea Gerta had brought. Dr. Mortimer took a cup of the steaming liquid as well, but he set it down next to his brandy snifter and spoke again.

"You must start at the beginning and include every detail you can." He settled back in his chair, but in spite of his relaxed posture, his eyes still smoldered.

Alexandra had scarcely started when Gerta reappeared at the door. "Excuse me, Doctor," she said, addressing Dr. Mortimer. "There is a gentleman at the door who says his name is Forsythe. He claims to be an associate of your guest and insists that he must be allowed entrance."

Dr. Mortimer turned to Alexandra. "Do you know this man?"

"I . . . Yes, of course," Alexandra said, deciding to minimize the awkwardness of the situation as much as possible, although she was seething with anger at Nicholas for putting her in such a position.

"Then show him in." Dr. Mortimer sounded annoyed.

Nicholas entered looking handsome and very much the elegant aristocrat with his tall, well-built frame and his expensively tailored suit. He went immediately to the alienist with his hand extended. "Dr. Mortimer, I can't tell you what an honor it is to meet you at last." He spoke without feigned effusiveness and with a quiet confidence.

"Indeed," Dr. Mortimer said in his icy voice.

"I must tell you I was impressed with your work on the McGarry case. Quite innovative. I believe you may have changed one aspect of medical jurisprudence forever, that which deals with the criminally insane." Still with his sincere, matter-of-fact tone.

"Well, now, that's a rather bold statement." Dr. Mortimer's voice had lost some of its chill.

"Nevertheless, it's true. As I said, your thinking is quite innovative."

"You are perhaps a member of the queen's bar?" Mortimer asked. "I understood you were Dr. Gladstone's assistant."

"Yes, I am," Nicholas said, leaving it unclear to which title he was making claim, then turned and acknowledged Alexandra for the first time. "I do hope you will forgive me for being late, Dr. Gladstone. The errand you sent me on took a bit longer than I expected."

Alexandra could only stare at him, in awe of his charming charade. She had not, of course, sent him on any errand at all.

Nicholas seated himself on the settee next to Alexandra, so close that his thigh pressed ever so slightly against hers. "Please, do go on with what you were discussing," he said.

"Dr. Gladstone was about to tell me the details of the case at hand," Dr. Mortimer said.

Nicholas turned to her and gave her a most annoyingly innocent little encouraging smile. Alexandra had to struggle to keep from rolling her eyes. Instead, she took a breath, turned her attention back to Dr. Mortimer, and told him about the gory murders of Ben Milligan and of the stranger, including how the bodies were found and how the heart of each had been removed, the stranger's with less expertise. When she had finished, Dr. Mortimer sat silently musing for several seconds, a thumb and forefinger stroking his beard while he stared into nothingness. Nicholas, in the meantime, was on his best behavior. He sat quietly listening, pretending he had heard it all before. Finally Dr. Mortimer spoke.

"This last murder, the stranger, I mean, you say that one occurred while the imbecile, young Lucas, was in gaol?"

"Yes," Alexandra said. "That's why Constable Snow released him. It was obvious that he could not have committed the murder while he was in gaol, and that he, therefore, was not likely to have committed the others either."

"But that was the one that was different, wasn't it? The other mutilation was more expertly done." Dr. Mortimer seemed to be thinking aloud rather than addressing Alexandra.

"Are you suggesting that Lucas could have killed the first victim?" She had read the paper Mortimer had authored which Snow had given her. His theories on the criminally insane, as she understood them, would not have indicted Lucas.

Dr. Mortimer brought his attention back to her. "It's possible the imbecile could have done it. The second murder could have been someone trying to mimic the killer of the first victim."

Alexandra shook her head. "I can't imagine who—"

"The imbecile's mother, perhaps? You said she was extremely protective of her son."

Alexandra felt a sudden empty chill, mingled with hot anger. She put her teacup on the table. "Excuse me, Dr. Mortimer," she said as she stood. Nicholas immediately stood as well. "I'm afraid I'm wasting the time of both of us. If you can have your carriage—"

"Sit down, please, Dr. Gladstone." Dr. Mortimer made no attempt to stand in deference to her gender.

"Your accusations, sir, sound like nothing more than the superstitious talk I hear at home from—"

"I said sit down, please, Dr. Gladstone." His voice was forceful and commanding, rather like a parent scolding a naughty child. Alexandra, acutely aware of Nicholas looking at her, did not sit, but she stopped speaking and stared at Dr. Mortimer.

"I am not accusing anyone, miss," he said. "I am merely allowing myself to consider all possibilities. If you can keep an open mind, perhaps you can aid me in this."

Alexandra had always considered herself to be openminded, but now she felt chastised, and her face burned with embarrassment. She sat down again. "I apologize, sir. Of course I can keep an open mind." Nicholas once again sat beside her, even closer this time. Was he being protective?

Dr. Mortimer ignored her apology and continued as if there had been no interruption. "Tell me, please, if you will, why you think Lucas is not a worthy suspect."

"He's very kind. Just not the sort. He cries when an animal dies." Alexandra knew that fell short of being the kind of intelligent, analytical answer Dr. Mortimer was seeking. She was, in fact, beginning to feel like an imbecile herself.

"Do you agree, Mr. Forsythe?" the doctor asked.

"What? Agree? For the most part, yes."

"Um-hum," Dr. Mortimer said and turned his attention back to Alexandra. "And his mother? Just not the sort either, I suppose."

"No," Alexandra said in what was almost a whisper.

"It seems you feel some particular need to protect these two, Dr. Gladstone."

Alexandra hesitated a moment, trying to collect herself. "Life has not been easy for Gweneth Pendennis," Alexandra said at length. "She has never been married. As I'm sure you can imagine, having a son out of wedlock has made her suspect of everything from madness to witchcraft, as well as immorality. And the fact that her son is an imbecile only adds to suspicion." She hoped neither of the men noticed the slight tremble in her voice.

"But you don't believe she is guilty of any of those things," Dr. Mortimer said.

"Of course not."

"Not even immorality?"

"Perhaps she made a mistake once, but I do not believe that necessarily constitutes a state of permanent immorality." Alexandra felt as if her lungs could not take in enough air. "In any case, immorality does not constitute insanity."

"And you, Mr. Forsythe?"

"Oh, I quite agree!"

Dr. Mortimer was silent for a moment, stroking his beard again, thinking. He picked up his brandy snifter and stared at the amber liquid in the bottom, then set it down again without tasting it. "It would appear," he said, breaking his silence at last, "that these murders are indeed the work of a homicidal maniac, just as Robert suggested." He glanced up at Nicholas and Alexandra again. "There is an erroneous belief among the public, however, that a homicidal maniac is easily distinguished from a sane person. I must tell you that is not necessarily the case. I remember a similar case I read about that took place in Paris. A man horribly mutilated. The killer was never found. The reason, I believe, is because the police were looking for someone who was obviously insane. A maniac who commits this kind of crime could be a person you see every day in the most mundane and ordinary circumstances. But hidden in the brain," he continued, "is the impulse to kill. It is the root of that impulse we must search for."

"You are referring to some malformation of the brain, perhaps?" Alexandra asked.

"No, I am not," Mortimer said. "I'm afraid it is much more complicated and—shall we say—more disconcerting than a physical abnormality."

"Disconcerting?" Alexandra asked. She was grateful that Nicholas was, so far, keeping his mouth closed.

"It is my belief," Dr. Mortimer said, "that a homicidal maniac can be made by his environment. Such a person, as I suggested, appears to be sane, and it is precisely that very fact that is so disconcerting to most people."

"Please explain," Alexandra said.

"My dear, it is certainly upsetting, if not absolutely frightening, to most people, that a person who appears to be as sane as they are is able to commit such heinous crimes. It makes us feel vulnerable, not just to the murderer, but to our own natures."

"A sane person doesn't kill people randomly." Alexandra's voice was insistent.

"Oh, it isn't random at all. Each killing is done for a very specific reason—the same reason in both of the Newton cases, I daresay."

"The same reason?" It was Nicholas who spoke, in a voice that was vaguely intimidating. Obviously he had kept quiet as long as he could. "Isn't it rather a big step to assume that both victims were in some way guilty of the same offense against the killer?"

"Indeed it would be," Mortimer said, "but the killer most likely is not concerned with the *guilt* of each victim. She most likely sees her victims only as the embodiment of what she fears or hates."

"She?" Alexandra said. "Are you still insisting Gweneth is the killer?"

"Ah, there is your protective nature showing itself again," Dr. Mortimer said. Alexandra thought she detected the slightest hint of a condescending smile on his lips. "Let us indulge in an exercise of the intellect and consider Gweneth for a moment." He stood, paced to the fireplace, and rested his arm on the mantel, stroking his beard for a moment again. "First let us look at the victims. What traits do they have in common?"

"They are both male," Nicholas said.

"Indeed. Anything else?"

Alexandra was momentarily too angry with Nicholas for bullying his way in to respond. She tried to glare at him, but he was, or at least pretended to be, oblivious of it.

"Anything else?" Dr. Mortimer said again.

Alexandra realized that Nicholas was silent because he had just given away the extent of his knowledge. "They are both of the approximate same age," she said, not sure where this was leading.

"Ah," Dr. Mortimer said. "How old?"

Nicholas looked at her as expectantly as Dr. Mortimer, waiting for her answer. "Middle-aged," she said, still not following his logic.

Dr. Mortimer paced back to his chair, but he remained standing and turned to the two of them again. "Let us continue this intellectual exercise. Let us say that the father of Gweneth's son was approximately the age of the victims. Let us assume, for the sake of the exercise, that she had a reason to hate this man."

"Perhaps she blames him for siring an imbecile on her," Nicholas said, getting into the game again.

"Very good," Dr. Mortimer said.

"Or she was angry because he didn't want the child," Alexandra said, aware that she was visibly shaking.

Dr. Mortimer nodded.

"Or," Nicholas added, once again in his barrister's voice, "he forced himself on her. Raped her. Hurt her badly. And repeatedly."

"Excellent!" Dr. Mortimer said with enthusiasm. "It is my belief that if such violence is perpetrated on a person repeatedly, and especially during childhood, then something goes awry in the person's mind, or soul if you will, and he or she becomes obsessed with correcting or righting the wrong or with gaining revenge. I also believe the maniacal killer may often enjoy the power of being able to manipulate the public and becomes upset if someone else is blamed for the crimes. It's as if they enjoy the notoriety, even if anonymously. I also have concluded from studying other cases, that the maniacal killer will break the pattern and kill outside of his chosen pattern, only if he thinks someone is coming close to uncovering the truth."

"That is very interesting, Dr. Mortimer, but most of what you described about Gweneth is pure speculation," Alexandra said.

Dr. Mortimer nodded. "Indeed it is. As I said, it was a mental exercise. I used the scenario merely to illustrate how a so-called homicidal manic may act. We could, of course, choose another suspect. Perhaps your nurse. Nancy, is it? Or the one you call Polly?"

"Must it be a woman?" Alexandra was growing more and more unsettled.

"Of course not. We could use any man you suggest as the suspect and repeat the exercise. You must understand, of course, that these recent murders may not be the first ones the killer has committed, and I will tell you most assuredly, they will not be the last unless you apprehend him or her soon. And remember this: The only other reason the murderer may have to kill is if she thinks you are coming close to unmasking her."

Alexandra stiffened. "Or him." There was an unpleasant edge to her voice, and she was aware of Nicholas's hand covering hers.

"You've been very kind and very helpful, Dr. Mortimer," Nicholas said, helping Alexandra to her feet. "But we really must be going. It's quite late, and I'm afraid we've disturbed you too long." He was leading her firmly toward the door, and Alexandra was chagrined to realize he was hurrying her away before she embarrassed both of them.

12

Alexandra was very much aware of Nicholas sitting across from her as they rode together in his carriage toward Kensington. She was even more aware of the silence between them, so thick it seemed to have clabbered. She found it impossible to speak, however, since she was angry with both him and herself. She was angry with him for intruding on her private affairs that had brought her to see Dr. Mortimer and angry with herself, as well as embarrassed, for her bad behavior, which made her appear not only petulant but, she feared, unintelligent.

Finally, it was Nicholas who broke the heavy silence. "I say, you're rather quiet tonight, aren't you?"

"Am I?" In spite of all, she could not yet quell her petulance.

Nicholas frowned at her. "I should think you'd want to discuss the case in light of all that Dr. Mortimer said."

"The case, Mr. Forsythe, is not your concern."

He raised an eyebrow. "Still peevish, I see."

She had just turned her face toward the curtain, open to the gathering lamplight of the city, but she quickly returned her gaze to him. "I beg your pardon."

"Of course you're angry with me for asserting myself and showing up uninvited. I expected it, but I should have thought you'd have gotten past that by now."

"It seems to be your habit, Mr. Forsythe, to assert yourself at all times where and when you will, in the belief that anyone who is annoyed will get past it, eventually. Rather bad behavior, I should say." Once again she tried to turn her face to the open window curtain.

"Speaking of bad behavior . . ."

She returned her gaze to him so suddenly and with such intensity that it appeared to startle him, causing him to stop in mid-sentence. "I know what you're going to say," she said, aware that her cheeks were blazing with embarrassment and emotion. "That I behaved badly as well. There is something you don't understand . . . that I can't." She lowered her eyes, knowing she was being foolishly defensive. "I'm sorry, I hope I didn't embarrass—"

"I was going to say, speaking of bad behavior, I'm afraid my behavior as a host at luncheon with you and Miss Nightingale was less than stellar."

She found she couldn't speak. She could only look at him in silence.

"You didn't embarrass me," he added quietly. "Or anyone else."

Except myself, she wanted to say, but still she could not speak.

Nicholas, too, was quiet for a moment before he spoke. "Perhaps a nice dinner would relax both of us. I know a wonderful place where . . . A *light* dinner, I mean. I know your custom is to avoid a heavy meal in the evening, so perhaps—"

"I should be happy to have dinner with you, Mr. Forsythe," Alexandra said. She had found his eagerness to put her at ease disarming. The least she could do was show some civility and accept his invitation.

Nicholas smiled and glanced quickly behind the curtain. "We're almost home. If you'd like a moment to change, I can meet you downstairs in half an hour."

She returned his smile, then allowed him to help her out of the carriage. He had a way of making her relax. If there was harm in that, it would be her own fault. Experience had taught her that.

She was grateful for the half hour he'd suggested before they meet downstairs. It would give her time to collect herself, to try to come to terms with her own childish behavior. She had no intention of changing clothes and preening in front of a mirror. There was nothing wrong with the linen dress she was wearing. The only thing she would concede to was to splash some water on her face.

She was blotting the water off with one of the finely embroidered linen towels the maid had provided when she caught sight of the green satin faille gown she'd spied earlier when she'd pulled her light linen suit from her trunk. She'd been annoyed at first that Nancy had been foolish enough to pack it, but this time she couldn't resist a closer look. After all, the fabric did have an uncommon richness to it, rather like the inviting depths of a shady forest. She allowed her fingertips the slightest touch of a sleeve, and they were met with a cool seductive feel of satin. The sensation radiated up her arm and made her shiver. She stroked the fabric with her entire palm, and then, in spite of herself, she slowly pulled the dress from where it nested in the trunk and held it in front of her as she gazed at herself in the mirror.

The woman whose reflection she saw surprised her. She

had never noticed that her eyes were quite so large and round and precisely the color of the dress, nor that her skin was a paler shade of the ecru lace, nor that the two colors together gave her auburn hair a glint of fire. Turning away from the mirror, she tossed the dress back into the trunk, where it settled with a swish, half in and half out. She was about to leave the room, prepared to wait in the drawing room for the rest of the half hour they'd agreed upon, when the dress caught her attention again. She stared at it for several seconds before she began frantically unbuttoning the jacket of her linen suit. She flung it aside, stepped out of her skirt, and had just pulled the lovely green frock over her head when there was a knock at the door and Broomsfield stuck her head inside.

"Oh, miss! Why didn't you call? Here, let me help you with that," she said, hurrying to smooth the skirt of the dress and to button the tiny buttons in the back. Before Alexandra could protest, Broomsfield had led her to the dressing table and forced her into the chair with a gentle shove. Her fingers flew about her head at what seemed to be blinding speed before she stood back and held the end of the brush to her chin in a pensive pose. "There we are!" she said.

Alexandra was stunned. Her hair had been pulled up and then allowed to fall in a cascade of curls at the back of her head in a style far more worldly than she'd ever worn. Not even Nancy had ever wrought such work.

"You don't like it." The maid looked as if she might burst into tears.

"Of course I like it," Alexandra said quickly. "It's . . . it's lovely, really. I've never . . . well, I've never seen anything quite like it."

Broomsfield's face changed itself into giddy relief. "It is lovely, isn't it? Master Forsythe will find you irresistible, I'm . . ." Her eyes widened for a moment as if she was surprised at her own breach of propriety, then she looked down at her hands, which were clasped in front of her.

Alexandra stood and turned to her, placing a hand on her shoulder. "Thank you, Broomsfield. You have quite literally transformed me." Her words brought a timid smile from the maid, and she followed Alexandra out of her room, fussing with the drape and folds of the rustling green skirt all the way to the top landing.

Nicholas was waiting in the front hall, seated beneath one of the portraits of an austere military figure from another century. He stood as soon as he saw her and didn't take his eyes from her as she descended all the way to the bottom of the stairs. "I've never seen you so . . . lovely," he said, as if he wasn't sure of the word. "May I?" He took the light shawl she carried on her arm and placed it around her shoulders, then offered her his arm.

He was dressed impeccably in trousers and matching coat of fine black wool. His white shirt smelled of starch with a hint of musk. The whiteness of it provided an intriguing contrast with the swarthy skin of his face and the intense blue of his eyes.

It was a short drive to the crowded restaurant Nicholas had chosen, and when they were led to their table by the maître d', she was aware of dozens of eyes following them. In spite of a new measure of self-confidence the dress had given her, she had no doubt that Nicholas was more likely the focus of their gazes, since he was undoubtedly well known by most of them, judging by the nods and murmured greetings he returned as they made their way to their table.

Nicholas ordered wine as soon as they were seated. Alexandra was glad to be handed a menu—anything to divert her mind from the eyes she still felt upon her back where the dress dipped to a V deep enough to reveal most of her shoulders. The menu was in French and written in an elaborately swirling cursive that, to Alexandra, seemed affected.

"May I suggest the veal?" Nicholas said, leaning toward her. "It's cooked with onions and tomatoes and garlic and covered with mushrooms."

She recognized it as his attempt to save her an embarrassment if she couldn't read the menu. In spite of the fact that she knew good manners would require her to accept his suggestion, she was not fond of veal. And in spite of the fact that she knew she was showing off, she told him, in French, that she preferred *le poisson cocote*.

He laughed. "There is, as always, more to you than meets the eye," he said.

"Not at all," she said, with a little laugh of her own. "I'm simply being arrogant and vaunting."

"It's good to see you relaxed. It was obvious Dr. Mortimer's hypothesis about Mrs. Pendennis made you uncomfortable," Nicholas said.

"It's Miss Pendennis, not Mrs.," Alexandra said, growing serious again. "And yes, the hypothesis was disturbing, and my behavior, I'm afraid, embarrassing."

"I can understand how it would feel to face even the suggestion of a friend's guilt in those circumstances."

She didn't tell him that Gweneth Pendennis was not really what one would call a friend, but that she felt a kinship with her that was more profound than mere friendship. There was no need in complicating what was supposed to be a relaxing evening. Instead she smiled benignly as he tasted the wine the steward had brought and nodded his approval. When the wine was poured,

Nicholas raised his glass. "To your career, Dr. Gladstone," he said.

Alexandra picked up her own glass and touched his before she tasted the wine. It was feathery dry on her tongue. "I'm afraid I've never had anyone toast my career before," she said.

"And why not? It's what drives you. It's the center of your life, is it not?"

She looked at him a moment before she answered. She was accustomed to veiled remarks about the importance she attached to her career, spoken as a transparent cover to disapproval—a rebuke that a husband and children were not the center of her life, as should be the case for every woman. Yet she could not detect the sarcasm in Nicholas. "Yes," she said at length. "It is the center of my life."

"It's the people—your patients . . . No, they're not just your patients, they're your friends, who make it important to you. That's why you're so concerned by these recent events." He looked at her as if she were some particularly arcane puzzle he'd been given to solve.

"These recent events, as you call them, are unspeakably horrific, Mr. Forsythe. They would be cause for anyone's concern."

"Indeed," he said, setting his own glass aside. "And you are afraid. In more ways than one."

"What do you mean?"

"Dare I speculate that you're afraid you know who the killer is? And that's what is distressing you?"

She looked at him, partly surprised and partly relieved that this time he was not nearly as perceptive as usual. "If you're thinking I believe Gweneth Pendennis is guilty, then you are most certainly wrong, although I can understand how you might misinterpret my protectiveness toward her. It's just that the circumstances in which she finds herself have caused her a great deal of pain, and I wish to protect her from more pain."

"Even if she's guilty?"

"She is not guilty."

"You are certain?"

She hesitated to speak. She had inadvertently led herself into a quagmire again, and she wanted desperately to move away from the subject of Gweneth Pendennis. She could not allow him to guess that she felt a kinship with the woman because of her own past. How could she ever tell him that she had found herself pregnant at the age of nineteen and that she would have suffered the same shame as Gweneth had she not miscarried? How could she bare to live again the shock and then despair she'd felt by telling him that the man she loved had told her he could not marry her, and that he would not acknowledge the child. How could she speak aloud the hurt and grief that had caused her, or worse, the guilt she'd felt for being secretly glad to have lost the child a few weeks later?

"Forgive me, Dr. Gladstone. I see that I've upset you."

She had been looking away, staring at nothing, but his remark brought her gaze quickly back to him. She saw the way he studied her—curious, questioning, perhaps even suspicious. "It's a troubling situation," she said. "Frightening even."

"Of course," he said. "Perhaps we should talk of something else."

She managed a small laugh, forcing herself to find her way out of the morass she'd led herself into. "I know you well enough, Mr. Forsythe, to know how insatiably curious you are about the murders. You've found yourself a bone you won't easily let go of. Perhaps we should play Dr. Mortimer's little game—his intellectual exercise, as

he called it—and see if we can find a motive for someone
else."

"Really?" Nicholas said with genuine surprise. "Whom
do you suggest?"

"Why not me?"

"You?" He laughed. "You're joking, of course."

"I'm not."

"I don't see the point," he said.

"All right, then, we'll do someone else. Nancy, perhaps." She was working hard at keeping levity in her
voice.

"I don't think we should make light of this," he said.

She felt chastised by the look in his eyes as much as
his words.

"If we're going to play the game," he added, "we
should consider someone with a motive."

"Such as . . ."

"How about the apothecary's apprentice you mentioned."

"Clyde? What would be his motive?"

"You mentioned in your narrative to Dr. Mortimer that
you've speculated that Harry Neill and the others may
have been purposely infected with anthrax. With Harry
Neill out of the way, there's no one to run the apothecary
shop. Clyde could have seen it as a way for him to take
over and have a shop of his own, thereby circumventing
finishing his apprenticeship and having to hire on as an
assistant."

She toyed with her wineglass a moment. "But what
reason would he have to kill the others?"

Nicholas's brow furrowed in a pensive frown. "Perhaps
Clyde was careless and left some clue they stumbled
upon. Or perhaps they all witnessed his killing Harry."

"Even the stranger Polly found in the alley? Not very likely, is it?'

"Perhaps not," Nicholas said, frowning again.

"And it doesn't fit the prototype Dr. Mortimer described. Someone who kills for what the victims *represent* rather than for a self-aggrandizing motive."

Nicholas's frown deepened. "Must it?"

"I don't know," she said.

By that time their food had arrived, and their conversation stopped as the waiter arranged dishes on the table, including plates with beautifully presented entrées, the likes of which Alexandra had never seen. The taste, she soon realized, was equally remarkable. Except for the meal Polly had prepared for her, she had never tasted anything so exquisite.

Remembering that, she thought once again of Nancy and Polly and the boys back in Newton and found she still could not rid herself of the feeling that they were all in danger.

"Is something wrong?" Nicholas asked.

His question surprised her. She hadn't realized her concern was at all obvious. "No," she said, pretending to misunderstand. "The dinner is perfect. Thank you for asking me here."

"I wasn't asking about the food."

She looked up suddenly from her plate, and then down again. She didn't like the way he unnerved her.

"I was asking about you. But you're not used to that, are you? People asking about your welfare."

"It doesn't matter," she said, forcing herself to look at him.

"What?"

"It doesn't matter what I'm used to or not used to. You mustn't examine me too closely."

"And why not?" He looked at her steadily and seemed to have forgotten about his veal.

"Please don't pretend you don't know where this is leading."

He laughed and cut his veal without taking his eyes from hers. "One of the things I like most about you is that you are so direct. It's very seductive, you know."

"I'm not trying to seduce you, Mr. Forsythe."

He popped a morsel of veal in his mouth with his fork and smiled at her with his eyes as he chewed and swallowed, then, touching the napkin to his mouth, he said, "Of course not," and smiled again, this time with his mouth as he cut into one of the delicately browned potatoes on his plate. He was clearly enjoying himself.

Alexandra resisted the urge to defend herself verbally and placed a bit of fish on the back of her fork and brought it to her mouth. There was a long silence as they both ate their food. Nicholas was the first to speak. One word.

"Fearless."

Alexandra looked up at him. "Excuse me?"

"Fearless," he said again, showing her that smile that meant he was still enjoying himself. "That's what you are. Restrained, cool, and fearless."

"Is that a criticism?"

He studied her face a moment, as if he wasn't sure of the answer. "No, I don't think so," he said finally. "I dislike being with a woman whom I have to guard against trampling." Something came up in his eyes as he said that. It passed quickly, however, so that she was not sure it had been there at all. He looked at her again. "Things seem to be going badly with the Boers in the Transvaal," he said.

"What?" His sudden shift in the conversation struck her

as comical. She almost choked on a bit of the fried bread she'd been served with her meal and was forced to take a sip of wine.

"Sorry," he said. "I was just trying to change the topic to something benign. I didn't want you to be uncomfortable."

She lowered her eyes and placed the tips of her fingers to her lips to keep from laughing.

"There's nothing a man dreads more than having a beautiful woman laugh at him," Nicholas said.

She shook her head as she raised her eyes and tried to bite her lips to keep from laughing. "It's . . . it's just that you're trying so hard," she said. "We both are."

"If I'd known the war in Africa would strike you so funny, I'd have brought it up long ago."

"Am I really such a dreadful bore?" she asked.

"Dreadfully serious is all."

"I know."

"That's not necessarily a fault."

"I know."

Nicholas laughed and picked up his glass. "To dreadful seriousness," he said.

He made her laugh as well, and the conversation for the rest of the evening was much lighter. Nicholas, Alexandra realized, had a very clever way of putting her at ease. The relaxed mood lasted all the way home until they stood facing each other at the foot of the stairs.

"Thank you," she said. "It was a pleasant—no, it was a delightful evening."

He looked at her, his tall silk hat still cocked over one eye in a rakish way. He removed the hat and continued to look at her with a faint smile on his lips. "I'm still very curious, you know."

"Curious?" she asked.

"About that mask you wear. I hope you'll let me see behind it someday."

She felt that void in her chest. It frightened her a little that he would be so perceptive, but when she spoke her voice was even. "Good night, Mr. Forsythe."

He held her gaze with his own for the briefest of moments, and she thought at some point during that short time that he might kiss her, but he made no move, and she turned away and walked up the stairs.

Broomsfield came to help her undress, but she sent her away on the pretense that it was late and the maid needed her rest for her duties in the morning. The truth was, she wanted to be alone, to relive the evening. When she was in bed, however, her thoughts bumped against each other, bringing up memories not only of the pleasant and dangerously flirtatious conversation with Nicholas, but of his alarming perceptiveness and his rude encroachment on her visit with Dr. Mortimer, all that Mortimer had said, the intellectual game he had played and that she and Nicholas had replayed. She found it impossible to relax, because it was then that all that had happened in Newton came hammering back into her thoughts, along with her worry for Nancy and the others. And then there was the game again, with Dr. Mortimer's voice this time. *She most likely sees her victims only as the embodiment of what she fears or hates.*

Fear and dread suddenly replaced all of her aimless thoughts and she sat up in bed. She knew who the killer was, and she knew she had to get back to Newton before someone else was murdered.

13

Robin Foggarty was worried. He hadn't seen Nancy in more than two days. Not since shortly after Dr. Gladstone left for London. He and young Artie had been in the mews mucking out the little mare's stall when he last saw her. She'd stepped out of the door at the back of the house to fetch some herbs from her garden, and she'd waved to them and wished them a good morning, saying she was going to bake some chocolate biscuits later and would bring them some. That big beast of a dog, Zack, was right at her heels, sniffing at the herbs as if he knew as well as Nancy what they were and what ailments they would heal. The two of them had gone back into the kitchen, Nancy carrying a basket full of herbs, Zack following close behind.

Artie had seen her after that. He often grew restless before any of their work was done, and as he frequently did, he told Rob he was going to the cistern at the side of the house for a sip of water. He'd had his drink, all right, but then he'd wandered off, looking for something more amusing than mucking out stalls. He happened to be near the front of the house, he said, when he saw Nancy leave with that woman, Polly Cobbe, who visited sometime. He told Rob they both wore their bonnets and carried parasols, as if they were out for a stroll, and that Zack wasn't with them. At first, he'd been reluctant to admit having been in the front of the house and seeing the two of them, and Rob knew it was because he didn't want a scolding and his ears cuffed for slacking his duty. He'd finally admitted seeing them, however, when he became as worried as Rob that Nancy hadn't returned.

Rob didn't have the heart to scold him then, or to cuff his ears. In fact, he was finding it harder and harder all the time to lay even a finger on the boy. He was probably no more than ten years old, or maybe no more than nine, the way Rob figured it, and he didn't like to see the kid hurt—at his hands or anyone else's. Rob had taken young Artie under his care two years ago when they were both on their own at the waterfront and living off what they could steal. Artie was hardly more than a baby then, the way Rob remembered it. He was near starved to death when he first showed up, scared out of his wits. His trip down the coast from Colchester had been hard on him, but the poor kid hadn't known what else to do after his ma died, except to keep moving in search of food and away from trouble in the form of other boys who tried to abuse him in one way or another.

Rob had first seen the dirty-faced little boy at one of the piers being cuffed by an oysterman who'd caught him stealing part of his catch. Rob rescued him by trading him for a jug of whisky he'd stolen himself from the old man everyone knew as Old Beaty, a former oysterman who liked to hang out around the piers. He'd taken him back to his "family," a group of other boys who survived by theft. Most of that group was gone now—either dead or in chokey. He'd likely be there himself, along with little Artie, were it not for Nancy, who'd hired them both as stable boys for Dr. Gladstone, and for the good doctor herself, who'd let them stay in spite of the fact that Nancy had stepped out of bounds by hiring them without permission. Both women had been kind to him and little Artie, giving them a nice room above the stable and all the food they could eat, as well as a decent wage. Dr. Gladstone even let them eat and sleep in the house when there was a storm or one of them was sick and needed care. Rob had never known such kindness and, he suspected, neither had Artie. He'd lay down his life for either Nancy or the doctor.

"You are certain, are you, Artie, that Nancy never told you where she was going?" Rob had asked the question at least half a dozen times before, and he asked it again as he and Artie, along with Zack, sat in their quarters above the stable, dining on what was left of the boiled mutton they'd found in the larder inside the main house.

"I told ye, Rob, Nance acted like she never seen me. She was lookin' straight ahead like she wanted me to think she never knowed I was there. And before ye asks again, Polly never seen me for sure. And she never said a word, 'cept to Nance, and I knows not what she said on account of I couldn't hear it."

Rob was silent, trying to think it through. Since Artie hadn't mentioned at first that he'd seen the two of them leave, Rob had not suspected anything for a long time. Even when Nancy failed to bring their supper up as she usually did, he didn't question it, assuming she might have walked to the village to see a patient for Dr. Gladstone. It wasn't until he heard the beast howling to be let out of the house that he felt the first hint of concern. It wasn't like Nancy to leave Zack for so long. He'd expected to have to break a window to get inside to free the dog, but he was surprised to learn that Nancy had left the back door unlocked. Did that mean she had planned to come back right away? Or had she left it unlocked because she wanted him to get inside and find the message she'd written on a scrap of paper? At least he thought it was a message, but he wasn't certain, since he was unable to read anything except his own name, which he recognized at the top of the note. He'd picked up the paper and stuck it deep into a pocket. Later that night he'd pulled the paper out and stared at it for a long time as if he could somehow will the letters on the page to speak to him. Besides the note that seemed to call to him all night long in a language he couldn't understand, he'd had to listen to Zack howl most of the night because Nancy hadn't returned.

Now another night had passed, and they were well into another day, and she still hadn't returned. Then patients started showing up for the surgery hours, Kate with her baby, and Nell, the butcher's wife, and of course, farty old Mrs. Sommers. Dr. Gladstone wasn't due back for another day yet, so Rob had sent them all away, telling them to come back tomorrow. It was clear as the nose on a man's face that something was wrong with Nancy, though, and it was equally clear that something had to be done. Rob knew it was up to him to do it.

"Is she all right, Rob?" Artie asked. "Ye think she's run off?"

"I told you, I don't know." Rob stood and cleared the table of the dishes, dumping them all in the big basin to be washed later. His response had come out sounding angry, and he immediately regretted it. Little Artie was as

worried as he was, and it would do no good to be cross
with him. He picked up a morsel of the mutton that had
fallen on the table and tossed it to Zack, who sat in front
of the door. The dog sniffed at the meat, but didn't eat it.
He had eaten very little since Nancy left.

"What should we do, Rob?" Artie's voice was choked.
He was having a hard time keeping the tears back. When
Rob didn't answer, he spoke again in a small, frightened
voice. "Maybe we should tell old Snow."

Rob glanced up at him suddenly. "The constable?" He
shook his head. "We ain't never had nothin' but trouble
with coppers, Artie."

"Then what? We got to do something."

Rob tried to ignore Artie's large glistening eyes pleading with him. He threw the last spoon in the basin and
walked to the window, his back to Artie. What should he
do? Maybe the kid was right. Maybe they ought to talk
to the constable. But Rob still couldn't get it out of his
mind that a policeman equaled trouble. What would old
Snow do anyway, if he did somehow know Nancy was
missing? Look for her, of course. Where? Artie had said
they were headed toward the village. Maybe they could
ask people there if they'd seen them. They could even
take Zack along. Dogs had good noses on them. He could
sniff her scent.

He turned around in time to see Artie quickly brush a
tear from his pale, frightened face. "Don't worry, kid," he
said. "I've got a plan." When he saw Artie's face brighten,
he didn't have the heart to tell him what a feeble plan it
was.

Alexandra was relieved to see that Nicholas had not yet
gone to bed. He was standing by the window at the top

of the landing, staring out at the stars that nibbled holes in the darkness above his garden. He had removed his coat and loosened his cravat and stood there in a stance that was relaxed but oddly melancholic as he smoked a cigar. He turned around abruptly when he heard the soft pad of her bare feet on the wooden floor.

"Dr. Gladstone? Is something wrong?"

She was struck by how libertine he looked. The same hand that held his cigar also held a glass of some amber liquid, which she judged to be whisky. "Yes," she said at length. "I'm afraid there is something wrong." He took a step toward her, his eyes full of concern. Before he could take another step, she said, "I know who the killer is."

His only sign of curiosity was a momentary rise of his eyebrows.

She wanted to tell him, to get it said and in the open, but in spite of the relatively warm night, she felt suddenly cold, and fear robbed her of her voice.

"You're shaking," Nicholas said. "I'll wake one of the servants to make you tea and—"

"No!" She sounded emphatic. "Don't awaken anyone. I should like to discuss this with you privately. Can we go downstairs?"

"Certainly. Let's go to the drawing room. . . ."

She sensed that he wanted to say more, specifically that he wanted to ask her again, whom, exactly, she thought was the killer, but he resisted and led her to the drawing room, taking pains to see that she was comfortable and that her shoulders were covered with a throw that had been draped across the back of one of the chairs. "All right now," he said, leaning forward when he had put out his cigar and seated himself across from her, "tell me, is it Polly?"

His question both surprised and unnerved her. "Why . . . would you suggest it's Polly?"

Nicholas shrugged slightly and leaned back in his chair. "It's just that Mortimer gave such a plausible motive for Miss Pendennis when he was conducting his 'mental exercise' as he called it, but you were emphatic in your belief that it couldn't have been she, so I started thinking that the same motive could apply to this Polly you told me about. She apparently hasn't had any illegitimate children, of course. At least you haven't mentioned any, but there are other reasons for women to hate men, aren't there? There are so many ways to abuse a woman—physically, sexually, perhaps even emotionally."

"But there is that possibility for any number of women. What made you choose Polly when you don't even know her?"

"Perhaps the fact that I don't know her is part of the reason I thought you might suspect her." He leaned all the way back in his chair and started to take a sip of his whisky, but he glanced at her again and asked, "Would you like a drink? Sherry, perhaps?"

"Nothing, thank you, and I don't know whether to think your statement is egotistical or irrational."

Nicholas set his drink aside. "It's neither. It's just that I've been to Newton-Upon-Sea enough to know that the population is relatively stable, and I daresay I've met most of the people in the town. Or a good many of them anyway. And the fact that these murders began only recently could mean it's someone new. Someone I don't know. Polly perhaps."

"Mr. Forsythe, not even I could possibly know all the new people who might come to town. I say your reasoning is unsound."

"Perhaps it is, but mind you, I said that was only part

of the reason." He set his glass aside. "And anyway, I
didn't say I suspected her as the killer, I was merely
guessing that you might. Suppose you tell me why you
suspect her."

"I didn't say it is she I suspect."

"But it is."

Alexandra was silent for a long moment, annoyed that
he would use such faulty logic to come to his conclusion.
Annoyed even more that, using that faulty logic, he had
guessed right. "All right," she said with reluctance. "Let's
say I do suspect her. Let's say that I agree with your
reasoning that she could possibly have an insane reason
to kill, as you suggested. I would then say, speculating
further, that her training as a nurse would give her some
understanding of surgical procedures so that she could,
possibly, remove the heart of her victims."

"But you say the last victim was mutilated in a more
inexpert way." Nicholas's words were spoken not as criticism, she realized, but as analysis.

"Yes. That's certainly difficult to explain."

"Could she have been in a hurry for some reason?"
Nicholas asked, leaning forward again.

"Of course she could have been," Alexandra said, "but
I can't quite work out the reason. Unless. . . ."

"Unless? You're on to something. What is it?" Nicholas
leaned forward even more eagerly.

"I was just remembering something Dr. Mortimer said
about how killers who murder a series of victims enjoy
the notoriety, even anonymously. So if—"

"Of course!" Nicholas interrupted, suddenly standing.
"If the suspicion was pointing to someone else—Lucas or
his mother—then the killer might feel compelled to do
something to remove the suspicion. Namely, kill again
when it could not have possibly been either of them."

"Exactly what I was thinking," Alexandra said, looking up at him. "But there's more."

"More?"

"I think so. I'm just not certain . . ."

"My god, Alexandra, what is it? Remember it's only a mental exercise. We don't have anyone on trial." Nicholas sat next to her on the settee. He was seemingly unaware that he had used her Christian name to address her, but the sound of it on his lips made Alexandra's heart beat a little faster.

"I . . . I'm not quite certain . . ." She hesitated a moment, willing herself to be calm. "It's just that I can't stop thinking about something Miss Nightingale said."

"About Polly?" Nicholas seemed puzzled, confirming what she had suspected all along—that he had not paid close attention to their conversation during lunch.

"Yes, remember she said she'd met Polly in Paris? And that she had been employed by Monsieur Louis Pasteur?"

"Mmmm, yes," he said, giving her further suspicion that he had no idea what she was referring to.

"Quite by coincidence, Dr. Lister mentioned Monsieur Pasteur's work on vaccines, which I am familiar with, of course, but I didn't know he was experimenting with anthrax vaccines."

Understanding shone in Nicholas's face. "My god! Polly could have had access to the germs."

Alexandra nodded, but she was silent again for a moment, trying to order her thoughts and to make sense of them. She glanced up at Nicholas. "Remember, I also said the third victim, Ben Milligan, survived."

"Yes, go on."

"Isn't it possible that when Ben survived, Polly resorted to strangulation to kill him."

"Of course!"

The two of them stared at each other silently for a moment before Nicholas spoke. "Nancy?"

"She is with Polly."

"God help us!" Nicholas whispered. "Dr. Mortimer said killers like that will kill someone who doesn't fit the description of their usual victim only if that person begins to suspect . . . And Nancy is clever enough . . ."

"And Polly is clever enough to know when Nancy works it all out."

"Then she is in danger." Nicholas said. He stood again, but Alexandra seemed unable to move. "We have to warn her. A telegram?"

Alexandra shook her head. "She may not be in a position to receive a telegram. And besides, that would risk someone else knowing the truth, someone else being in danger."

"Then we have to go," Nicholas said. "The next train leaves at five A.M. That's only a few hours from now."

14

The first thing to do, Rob decided, was to find a piece of Nancy's clothing so he could communicate to Zack that he wanted him to help find her. With Artie sticking close as jam on a scone, Rob went back inside the house and found one of Nancy's aprons in the kitchen and stuck it under the big dog's nose. Zack sniffed the apron and whimpered as he looked up at Rob.

"That's right, Zack, old boy, we both want Nance to come home, don't we?" Rob said. "Now, go find her." He pointed toward the front door in what he hoped was an encouraging gesture. Zack turned his big head in the direction Rob had pointed, then ambled toward the old-fashioned hearth and plopped himself down in his accustomed place. With a heavy sigh, he placed his head on his forepaws and looked up at the boys with large, liquid eyes and whimpered again.

"Damn you, Zack!" Artie said.

Rob jerked his attention to the boy. "Don't be swearin'
in Dr. Gladstone's house!"

Artie's face drained white, and he spoke in a frightened
whine. "But she ain't here . . ."

"Never you mind where she is, boy. Nance and the doc
don't fancy yer swearin'!" Rob saw the frightened tears
forming in Artie's eyes, but he turned away, too frightened himself to comfort him. "Now go get the leash for
the beast," he said over his shoulder.

"What?" Artie's voice trembled.

"The leash. For Zack," Rob said, turning back to Artie.
It would give the boy something to do while he himself
fought back his own despair. While Artie fumbled with
the leash, Rob crumbled the apron into a wad and stuffed
it under his arm. "Let's go," he said when Zack's leash
was secured to his collar. "You lead the way, Artie. Take
us in the direction you saw Nance and Polly walking."

"This way," Artie said when they were outdoors. He
pointed toward the path that followed the shoreline for a
short distance before it angled inland toward the heart of
the village. They had not had time to take more than a
few steps away from the house when they saw someone
walking toward them.

"It's the idjet," Artie said. There was no fear or disgust
in his voice, only resignation at being delayed.

As soon as Lucas spotted them, he bounded toward
them in his awkward, unwieldy gate, calling out to them.
"Where'd she go? Can I see her?" He stopped in front of
them, slack-jawed and breathing hard as his eyes darted
from one boy to the other.

"If ye come to see the doc, she ain't here," Rob said.

"Besides, surgery hours ain't 'til afternoon," Artie
added.

"She's gone, ain't she?" Lucas said. "Is she coming back?"

"The doc? Sure she is, Lucas," Rob said. "But not until later. I'll tell 'er to come by and see ye."

"No!" Lucas shook his head in an exaggerated movement.

Rob tried to move around him. "We got to be goin' now, Lucas. You come back later and—"

"No!" Lucas's voice was louder and full of agitation. " 'Tisn't Dr. Gladstone I wants, 'tis Nancy. She ain't comin' back, is she? I could tell, 'cause I seen 'er."

"You seen Nancy? Where?" Rob felt his heartbeat quicken. Lucas shrugged and kicked at a clod of dirt. Rob grabbed his arm. "Where?" Lucas looked at him with a blank expression for a moment before he spoke.

"Don't know."

Rob grabbed Lucas's thick arms and tried to shake him. "God damn you, where? Think!"

Lucas shook his head again and shouted back at Rob. "Don't know!"

Rob was about to spit a mouthful of curses at him when Artie intervened, trying to push him away from Lucas. "He don't understand, Rob. He just means he don't know where she is."

Rob glanced at the boy and back at Lucas, fighting to keep his anger and fear under control. He spoke to Lucas in slow, measured tones. "You said you seen Nancy. When, when did you see her?"

Lucas shrugged. " 'Twas in the daytime."

Rob's heart pounded even harder. "Yeah, 'twas daytime, Lucas. Where did you see her? Was she with someone?"

Lucas gave him his slack-jawed stare again, and Rob realized he had confused him by asking two questions at once. "Where did you see Nancy?" Rob asked again, speaking slowly, enunciating each word.

Lucas continued to stare for a moment, then pointed toward the path leading along the shoreline. "I think the other one hurt her," he said in a frightened voice.

"Who?" Rob asked, trying not to let his fear take control. "Who do you think hurt her?" She and Polly must have met some unsavory characters along the waterfront. Nancy should have been smart enough to know that area was not safe for women. He felt anger born of worry rise in his throat until he heard Lucas speak again.

" 'Twas Polly," Lucas said. "I seen 'er push Nancy. I wanted to help 'er, so I ran, but I fell down, and then I couldn't find 'em. Did she take Nancy away? Where is she?"

Before Rob or Artie could reply, another voice caught the attention of all of them. It was Kate Hastings coming up the path to the surgery with her sleeping baby swaddled in her arms.

"I must see Nancy," she said.

"Nancy ain't here," Lucas said before either of the other two boys could reply. "And Dr. Gladstone ain't either."

Kate gave Lucas a disdainful look. "I know the doctor's away. 'Tis Nancy I seek."

"The other one pushed 'er," Lucas said.

Kate ignored him and walked around him as she tried to make her way to the surgery door.

" 'Tis true, girl, Nance ain't here," Rob said.

She stopped and turned around slowly to face him. A look of recognition swept across her face. Rob knew the young woman had seen both him and Artie working around the house. "My baby," she said, looking down at the sleeping child in her arms, "she is improved, but I need more of the medicine the doctor gave her. She told me before she left that Nancy would give it to me."

Rob shook his head. "Come back tomorrow."

"I need it now!" Kate insisted, then added, "It's the nights that she worsens. The medicine helps her sleep."

Rob was about to tell her again to come back tomorrow, but he saw the dark circles under the girl's eyes and noted how she seemed to have grown thinner since the last time she was there, as if she had neither slept nor eaten. He sighed and shook his head in frustration. "Try the apothecary," he said, sounding angrier than he felt.

Kate looked at him with her tired eyes and spoke to him in her equally tired voice. "The apothecary is closed. Mr. Neill is dead."

It was Artie who spoke up this time. "No, it ain't closed. Clyde Wright runs it now." Artie had heard that bit of news at the same time Rob had when some of their old acquaintances at the waterfront told them. The story was that Clyde had broken the lock to the shop, which had been closed since Harry Neill's death, and that he had now set himself up as proprietor and apothecary, although Clyde denied it. He claimed that Harry Neill had left the shop to him. There was no way to prove whether or not that was true, since Harry's brother, Winston, his only living relative, was dead, too, and Harry had left no will. There was even some talk that taking over the shop had long been his plan, but that he'd grown tired of waiting for a legitimate opportunity and had done old Harry in. As much as he disliked Clyde, Rob still found it difficult to believe that he could have killed Harry. He'd died of some disease anyway, not murder.

"Clyde?" Kate said, interrupting Rob's thoughts. "The man makes my flesh crawl." Rob saw her look down at the sleeping baby in her arms again and once again sensed her fear and dread.

"All right," he said. "Me and Artie is going that way. We'll take you to the apothecary. You can ask 'im for the medicine Nancy gave you. 'E's sure to know what it is, ain't 'e? And 'e won't be givin' ye 'is disgustin' talk with us along," Rob said, not certain he believed it himself. He knew the girl would screw up her courage and face Clyde for the sake of her baby, but he hated to see the dread in her face. Hated, too, to think of her having to put up with Clyde's lewd looks and comments. It would sidetrack them on their search for Nancy, and he knew every minute was precious, but he couldn't think what else to do. The best he could manage was to send Artie, who still held Zack's leash, ahead with Kate and the baby while he held back a little with Lucas. He didn't want Lucas blurting out the fact that Nancy was missing and alarm Kate. There was no point in spreading the fear, not yet anyway, not until he had more time to sort things out and decide what to do. He'd managed to pull Artie aside long enough to whisper to him not to say anything to Kate about Nancy.

Kate and the baby, along with Artie and Zack, were already inside the apothecary by the time Rob and Lucas arrived, and Kate was trying to explain to Clyde the type of medicine she needed for little Alice. The shop smelled of earth and of green things, much like the doc's herb pantry, but there was a sour smell overlaying everything as well. As Rob looked around at the shelves and the counter, he noted the layer of dust and grime that covered everything. Clyde hadn't bothered to tidy up after he opened the shop, and if the dust wasn't enough testimony to that, the clutter of papers on the counter and the dirty stains on the floor were more than enough.

"Infusion of red clover? Sure, I've plenty o' that." He chuckled as he turned away toward a storage room. "And if me luck holds out, I'll be needin' all of it. Whooping cough is a contagion, 'tis. Every little snot-nosed brat in Newton will be needin' it." He chuckled again as he disappeared through the door and called over his shoulder to Rob and Lucas, "Be with you in a minute, boys." He was gone only a few seconds before he returned holding a jar filled with liquid. His face was stretched into a leering smile. " 'Tis a bit expensive, Katie, but there's a way you can reduce the price if yer willin'."

Kate responded by pulling Alice closer to her and trying to grab the jar from Clyde's hands. Zack growled, low in his chest, and his ears lay almost horizontal, but Clyde ignored him and laughed, holding the jar just out of Kate's reach. "Can you pay the price, Katie?"

"She'll pay sixpence," Rob said, taking a menacing step toward Clyde.

"Oh, but 'twill take more than sixpence," Clyde said, his gaze sweeping the length of Kate's body.

"She'll pay a sixpence!" Rob's words were clipped with anger.

Clyde turned his gaze from Kate to Rob, and his lecherous grin dissolved into a smirk. "This ain't none o' yer business, boy. Go on back where ye belongs, knee-deep in 'orse shit." He glanced at Artie and back at Rob. "What're you two doin' this far away from the doc's and Nancy's apron strings anyway?"

Before either Rob or Artie could answer, Lucas spoke and took a lumbering step toward Clyde. "They ain't here. Polly took Nancy away. Did she take the doctor, too?"

"What is this idjet talking about?" Clyde asked, looking at Rob.

"Polly pushed Nancy," Lucas said. "She was mean to her, and now she's gone. Did Polly take Nancy away? Will Nancy die like Seth's pigs?"

"Ye disgustin' idjet! Get out o' here 'afore old Polly

gets 'er hands on ye." Clyde finished off his cruel tease by trying to push Lucas toward the door, but Lucas wouldn't budge.

"Did she hurt Nancy?" Lucas seemed near tears, and Rob stepped forward to intervene by placing his hand on Lucas's arm, but Lucas brushed it off. "Did she?"

Clyde laughed his cruel laugh again. "What are ye worried about Nancy for? She can take care o' herself. Although 'tis true that Polly's a strange one. Used to tell me stories about killin' cats. Tortured 'em to death, she did. When she was nothin' but a wee child. Threw 'em into boiling water, she did, and laughed when she told me about it." He moved his face so close to Lucas their noses almost touched. "And I wouldn't be surprised if she wasn't the one what killed them pigs you love so much. What you been doin' with them pigs, idjet? What unnatural acts you been doin'?"

Lucas backed away from Clyde as tears and snot ran down his face. "Did she kill 'em? Did Polly kill the poor little pigs?"

Rob grabbed Lucas again, not giving him a chance to protest this time, and shoved him toward the door. "Go home, Lucas. Go home to your mama, and don't leave the house 'til I come tell you to. You, too, Kate. Go home!"

"Is Nancy all right?" Kate asked.

"I said go home, Kate!"

Kate snatched away the jar of herbs before she moved quickly across the room to follow Lucas out the door. Rob grabbed Artie's arm to pull him out.

Clyde ran after them. "What about the money she owes, you little thieves?"

Rob pulled a tu'pence from his pocket and threw it at

Clyde as he hurried away, herding the others in front of them.

"What's wrong?" Lucas asked, stumbling as he ran. "What's wrong?"

"Just run, Lucas," Rob shouted.

They'd run only a short distance when Kate slowed and then stopped, breathing hard and clutching her crying baby tightly to her chest. "I must rest," she gasped. "How could it be Polly what done all those dreadful things?" she asked, breathing hard as she looked up at Rob. "I seen 'er helping the doctor. She held Alice like she was 'er own. And I seen 'er help Lucas's ma that day at the market cross. Saved 'er from certain death, she did."

"I don't know how or why, Kate, but ye got to get home, and ye got to stay there to keep yer baby safe." He turned to Artie. "Take 'em home, Artie," he said, grabbing Zack's leash from him. "And take Lucas home as well. See that they all gets there safe, then you go home yerself. See that ye lock the doors, ye hear? I'll be along later."

"But Rob . . ."

"Do as I say, Artie. I needs ye to help me now."

Artie gave him a troubled look that lasted for only a second before he turned to Kate and Lucas. "Come on," he said. "I'll see that ye gets home safe."

Rob watched them go as Zack barked and tugged at his leash, wanting to go with them, but Rob held on tight. He was glad to have them all out of the way. He didn't understand the potential danger for them, he only knew it was real. No realer for anyone than for Nancy, though. He had to find her before it was too late. He pulled the wadded apron from under his arm and placed it in front of Zack's nose. The big dog sniffed, then looked up at Rob and whimpered.

*   *   *

Nell Stillwell, the butcher's wife, almost tore the door
from its hinges as she blasted into the constable's office.
She'd forgotten to put on the black patch she usually wore
to cover her dead left eye, and it glared and rolled at him
with milky foreboding in the split second before she
erupted into a frenzied barrage of words and advanced
toward where he sat at his desk. Her heavy boots left the
debris of the slaughtering pens on the floor, scattered like
odoriferous confetti. " 'Tis Nancy Galbreath! She's been
kidnapped by a madwoman, and I fear she's already dead.
Same as poor Ben Milligan. If she ain't dead, ye must
save 'er. And hurry! There's no time to waste." In front
of him now, she placed both of her large, bloodstained
hands on his desk and leaned so close to him he caught
the scent of pork kidney. "I tell ye, ye got to hurry, Snow.
They's no time to waste, and 'tain't that Pendennis
woman like we thought. 'Tain't a man either. 'Tis—"

"Sit down, Nell," Snow said in his quiet, commanding
schoolmaster's voice. He set aside the rather disturbing
document he'd just been reading and held his tall, thin
body very straight in his chair as he laced the long fingers
of his beautiful hands together and then rested his hands
with a menacing quietness on the desk in front of him.

Nell stopped speaking and stared at him with her one
good eye while the other one crept with a liquid stealth
backward into her skull, leaving a stark white hole. She
straightened herself and looked around for a chair. Finding one, she sat uneasily on the edge and kept her eye on
Snow.

When he spoke, his voice was icy. "All right, Nell,
what do you wish to tell me about Nancy Galbreath?"

" 'Twas Kate Hastings what told me she's missin', and

the boys, Rob and Artie, is out lookin' for her. The idjet, too, but they sent 'im home to his ma. 'Twas the idjet what seen Polly drag 'er off and told the boys, and 'twas Clyde Wright what told 'em how she likes to kill things and—"

"Just a moment, Nell. You're telling me Lucas Pendennis claims to have seen Polly Cobbe dragging Nancy away?"

Nell nodded. "I is."

"And what makes you think you can trust the word of the unfortunate boy who claims pigs speak to him?" Snow glared at her with his cold blue eyes.

Nell's hesitance was uncharacteristic. She was used to being in command. She might know her place among her betters, but no one, even the highest and mightiest, could truly intimidate her. Yet there was something about this long, tall stick of a man that could leave her stunned. "Rob thinks she took 'er too," she said finally, in a voice that was at least a little subdued. "And anyway," she added with more force as she fought her way out of the trance, "and anyway, Nancy ain't home. Hasn't been there for two days and two nights." She was standing now, completely herself again. "I think it best you do yer job, Constable. I think it best ye find Nancy Galbreath 'afore 'tis too late."

Constable Snow stood up from his desk, towering over Nell, who was no small woman in either height or breadth. "Thank you, Nell. I understand your concern, and I appreciate your vigilance." He took her arm and led her toward the door. "Dr. Gladstone will be back soon. Perhaps that will clear things up."

"But I don't see how—"

His grip on her arm tightened. "I'm sure Nancy hasn't gone far, Nell. You know how devoted she is to Dr. Glad-

stone and to her patients. I'm sure she's only seeing after
one of them." He led her with a firm hand out of the
building and closed the door. When he went back to his
desk, he picked up the document he'd been reading when
Nell had interrupted him. It was a telegram from Dr. Mortimer.

*"Have found information on unsolved murders in
France that fit description of Newton murders. One Polly
Cobbe, believed to be monomaniac, was suspect. Please
tell Gladstone."*

15

The train to Bradfordshire left London a few minutes before 5 A.M. and crept its way through the countryside at what seemed to Alexandra to be a painfully slow pace. Nicholas sat across from her, uncharacteristically quiet. She assumed it was a combination of the ungodly earliness of the hour the schedule had forced on them and his concern for Nancy, and possibly other potential victims, that made him untalkative.

Alexandra had not slept at all the night before. She had not, in fact, even bothered to go to bed. Instead, she'd spent the time pacing the floor and worrying about Nancy and the boys and wondering what could have happened to Polly that had twisted her mind into such a grotesque state. She thought of Polly's careful and tender care of the patients she'd helped, especially the Hastings baby. No one could have been more loving and careful. Neither could anyone have been kinder to Gweneth Pendennis, or for that matter, to Nancy. Perhaps her worry for Nancy and blame of Polly were completely misplaced. Polly couldn't possibly be a murderer, could she?

It could be a person you see every day in the most mundane and ordinary circumstances.

When Broomsfield had tapped on Alexandra's door at four o'clock that morning, she was sitting on her trunk, waiting. In spite of her sleepless night, she didn't feel tired then or even now that the journey was launched. But there was a persistent dull ache behind her dry, scratchy eyes.

"There is reason to hope that, whoever the killer may be, he or she won't break the pattern of killing only middle-aged men, and Nancy and your stable boys will be safe." Nicholas didn't look at her as he spoke but stared ahead with a fixed gaze. It was unclear whether Nicholas's statement was meant to comfort her or to comfort himself.

Alexandra glanced at him but found it impossible to reply. She turned her gaze out the window to hide her unease, and for one dreadful moment, it seemed to her that the train was moving backward. Lack of sleep was causing her to hallucinate. She glanced again at Nicholas, who had turned his full attention to her now.

"I'm quite convinced we have no reason to believe Nancy is in imminent danger. After all, she, as well as you, has been in Polly's presence several times without harm. Even slept in the same house. And we still don't know for certain she was responsible for all the killings, do we? Or even if she is, we don't know for certain that Nancy suspects her and is therefore in danger."

Alexandra closed her eyes and leaned her head against the back of her seat. "No, I suppose we don't know anything for certain." Too restless to keep her eyes closed, she stared at the ceiling. "But it's such a frightening likelihood, and I can't help thinking now that I may have made a mistake by advising against notifying Constable

Snow before we left. There might have been something he could do to protect Nancy." She raised her head to look at Nicholas again. "I was wrong to worry about panic spreading because telegraph operators would talk or that it could result in someone being wrongly accused."

"It does little good to talk about what might have been, Dr. Gladstone." There was an edge to his voice that surprised Alexandra. Worry or lack of sleep seemed to have transformed completely the flirtatious Nicholas of the night before.

"Is that your way of saying, 'I told you so'?"

"So you think of me as petty and vindictive."

"Vindictive is the last thing I would think of you."

He raised an eyebrow. "You were meant to deny both, you know."

She laughed. He was making an effort to suppress his dark mood, and it surprised her that he could evoke laughter from her at a time such as this. It would be easy—too easy—to rely on his ability to console her, too easy to like him too much. He smiled at her laughter and held her gaze a moment until she turned away.

Alexandra was still too restless to feel tired when the train pulled into the station at Bradfordshire. When she stepped to the door to exit the train, she was surprised to see the tall, slender form of Constable Snow among those waiting in the small crowd on the platform. He moved toward her and hesitated only slightly when he saw Nicholas behind her.

"Constable Snow, what a surprise!" Alexandra said as he advanced closer.

"I'm afraid I have some bad news," he said with only a cursory glance toward Nicholas.

Alexandra felt as if her blood had frozen. "It's Nancy,"

she said in a voice that was surprisingly calm, even to her own ears.

"What's happened?" Nicholas asked at the same moment Snow said, "I'm afraid she's disappeared."

"Disappeared? But how is that possible?" Alexandra felt and heard a roaring in her head, as if all her blood were rushing there.

"The boys are gone as well," Snow said. "There's no one at your house. Not even your dog, I'm afraid."

"But why . . . ?"

"Good god, man, tell us what this is all about," Nicholas said. "Why were you at Dr. Gladstone's house in the first place?"

Snow turned his attention to Alexandra as if she had been the one who had asked the question. "One of your patients, Kate Hastings, told Nell Stillwell that Nancy had left in the company of Polly Cobbe under somewhat suspicious circumstances, and Nell came to me. When I went to your house to investigate, I found the boys gone as well; then when I spoke to Kate, she seemed to think they'd gone searching for Nancy."

"Have you checked Miss Cobbe's lodging?" Nicholas asked.

Snow turned his icy glare on Nicholas. "I have."

"And . . . ?"

There was another moment of silence, just enough to fill Alexandra with cold fear. Finally he spoke. "I suggest you come with me to her room, Dr. Gladstone."

A horrible vision flooded Alexandra's senses—a vision of Nancy lying on the floor of Polly's dingy room above the tavern, her heart crudely severed from her body. She didn't remember agreeing to go with the constable or getting into his carriage for the ride back to Newton. She had only a vague memory of Nicholas sitting beside her and holding her hand as they made what seemed to be an interminable trip before they stopped in front of the constable's office and walked across the street to the tavern.

Nicholas's arm tightened around her shoulders as they stood in front of the door to what she presumed to be Polly's room and Snow inserted a key he must have obtained from the innkeeper. The door swung open, and she felt a draft of hot air at the same time a sour smell accosted her senses. She swept her gaze around the darkened room, and then again as her eyes adjusted to the dim light. There was no one there, no body lying on the floor.

"You have taken her away," she said in a voice that was strangely calm.

"I have taken no one away, Dr. Gladstone," the constable said. "There has been no one here for me to take away."

"But I thought—"

"Nancy and Polly are still missing?" Nicholas asked for her.

"Yes," Snow said. He pulled the telegram from his pocket and handed it to Alexandra. "Read this, Dr. Gladstone," he said, "and Mr. Forsythe should have a look at it as well."

Alexandra read Dr. Mortimer's message confirming what she already suspected. Seeing the alienist's validation served only to frighten her more. When she handed the telegram to Nicholas, he read it quickly then spoke to Snow.

"You've just handed me her defense."

Snow nodded. "She will not likely hang for her crimes."

"Criminal insanity will be her *defense*," Nicholas said. "It is another matter to prove it."

"And first I must build a case against her," Snow said

as he made his way to a window on the opposite side of
the room. He pushed back a faded curtain to allow more
light to enter then turned toward a table that held several
bottles, a rather expensive microscope, a few books, and
some test tubes. "I'd like you to examine the contents of
these containers, if you will, Dr. Gladstone."

Alexandra walked to the table and looked at all that
was on it. Just as Snow was about to pick up one of the
jars, which contained a gel-like substance, Alexandra
placed her hand on his arm to stop him. "I suggest you
not touch anything, Constable."

His eyes met hers briefly, and he moved his hand back.
"Can you examine all of this here, or do you wish to take
it to your own laboratory?" he asked.

She glanced at the table again and particularly at the
microscope. "I shall be able to do quite well here. This
equipment is superior to mine."

"Then I shall leave you to your work," he said.

"But what about Nancy and the boys? And Zack?" Alexandra called to his back as he started to walk away.

Snow turned around slowly. "The search will continue,
of course."

Alexandra took an anxious step toward him. "Where . . .
how will you—"

"Please try not to worry, Dr. Gladstone. I shall continue
my inquiries, and I assure you I shall work diligently."
He turned away again, and Nicholas followed him to the
door and closed it after he'd left.

"Is there anything I can do to help?" Nicholas asked
when the constable was gone.

"I'm . . . I'm not sure," she said, trying to compose herself. She looked around the room, hoping to convince herself that she could trust the constable to find Nancy and
the others. "But mind you, don't touch anything," she

said, pulling on the soft kid gloves she used for traveling, knowing full well they would be no good to her after this.

"Don't touch anything? You surely don't believe the entire room is contaminated."

"The point is, I don't know what is contaminated. It's possible even the very air we're breathing could be poisoned. There is much we don't know about contagions."

A troubled look crossed Nicholas's face. "Contagions?" His gaze moved around the room. "In here?"

Alexandra seated herself in front of the microscope and carefully placed a minute amount of the contents of one of the jars on a slide. "As I said, I don't know. I just have to have a look at . . ." She turned her gaze to Nicholas. "Why don't you put on your gloves and have a look around. Perhaps there'll be something out of the ordinary." Her thought was to keep him busy so she could concentrate on what she was doing.

She returned her attention back to the microscope and was only dimly aware of Nicholas moving away. She didn't realize how long she'd been looking at the long, rod-like molecules until Nicholas moved behind her and leaned over her shoulder.

"What have you found?" he asked.

"I don't have my reference books here to compare what I see, but I'm almost certain this is anthrax."

Nicholas nodded. "Just as we speculated."

She turned her eye back to the scope. "It appears . . ."

"She came here planning this?" Nicholas said, sounding as if he couldn't believe it himself.

Alexandra shook her head. "I don't know that she planned anything, but it's possible that when Polly stopped working in Pasteur's laboratory and left Paris, she brought these specimens with her. She would have understood how to keep them under control until she needed them."

"So she was responsible for the anthrax deaths!"

"I'm afraid so."

"But why did she choose Newton?"

"I'm not certain she chose Newton," Alexandra said. "It's possible she just happened to come here and saw her opportunity after she arrived."

"Opportunity?"

"Men," Alexandra said. "Men of the right age who would be her victims. That is, if Dr. Mortimer's theory is correct."

"Good lord!" Nicholas looked down at his gloved hands and held them out from him as if he feared contamination. He returned his gaze to Alexandra. "But if she used the contagion on her victims, why did it work one time and not another?"

Alexandra stood and carefully removed first one glove and then the other. "I can only guess, Mr. Forsythe. But extrapolating on the theory of vaccination and immunization, it is possible that some men in this agrarian area have a natural immunity, or at least some resistance to the anthrax germ. Perhaps others have not had the opportunity to develop the immunity. It's possible a natural immunity kept Lucas from contracting it when he played with the pigs. I don't know. There's much we don't know."

"She must have brought the disease to the pigs as well," Nicholas said. "Why?"

"Again, I don't know. It may have been accidental. It may have been meant only for men."

"Interesting. But how do you suppose Polly was able to contaminate her victims without contaminating herself? Had she developed an immunity herself?"

"It's possible," Alexandra said, "but I think it's more

likely she'd learned how to avoid contamination when she worked in the laboratory."

"Still, it's difficult to see how she could have caused her victims to come in contact with the germ."

"I'm not quite sure how she did it, but she's rather bright, you know. She could devise something cunning, I'm certain." Alexandra stood and moved away from the table and the microscope. "I suggest we leave now, Mr. Forsythe. The sooner we're out of here, the more likely we are to avoid contamination."

"Don't you think we should have another look around first?" Nicholas asked.

Alexandra was surprised at his reluctance to leave. "Of course not. Constable Snow asked me to examine those specimen, and given what I found, that's quite enough reason to leave."

"But it's not enough to charge her with murder," Nicholas said, looking around as he moved away from her.

Impatience burned in Alexandra. She felt an uncontrollable urge to do something to find Nancy and Zack and the boys. "Mr. Forsythe, you may stay here if you like, but I'm not—"

"Just a moment," Nicholas said, holding up a hand. "I just want to have a look at this shelf of books and then see what's on the other side of that door over there, and I strongly suggest you don't leave without me."

"There is no reason why I should require your presence, Mr. . . . ." She stopped speaking, realizing how foolish her statement was. Perhaps there was good reason not be alone, given the fact that Nancy and the others had disappeared. In spite of what Nicholas had said earlier, it was obvious to her that it was no longer only middle-aged men who were in danger. "Oh, for heaven's sake!" she said, as angry with herself as she was at Nicholas. She

stormed to the door Nicholas had indicated and jerked it
open. "I'll have a look in here if it will satisfy you enough
so we can . . ." No further sound would come from her
throat. She could only stare in horror.

In front of her, placed in neat rows on shelves and
supported by strings from the ceiling were the skeletons
of seven cats.

16

"Dr. Gladstone, is it?"

Alexandra recognized Polly's voice and whirled around to face her. Their eyes met, and Alexandra felt as if she'd been swallowed whole by cold fear itself. Her heart refused to beat until she felt Nicholas beside her, and then it seemed that her heart pumped too wildly.

"I must say I'm surprised to see that you're so rude and inconsiderate," Polly said, moving closer to the two of them. "I certainly never entered your house uninvited, did I? Nor did I presume to riffle through your personal belongings." She assumed a dour expression. "I'm not only surprised, I'm disappointed in you, as well." She shook her head in false distress. "What did I do to deserve this? Didn't I give you help when you needed it? Didn't I take care of poor Nancy as long as I could?"

"Where is Nancy?"

Alexandra was surprised to hear that it was Nicholas's voice asking that question and not her own.

Polly turned her attention to him. "Who are you? And what are you doing here?" There was a menacing note to her voice.

"We are here at the request of Constable Snow," Nicholas said before Alexandra could speak.

"Indeed!" Polly returned her gaze again to Alexandra. "And did you find what you were looking for?"

"You must know, Polly, how dangerous it is to have these anthrax specimens in your possession," Alexandra said.

"Anthrax?" For a moment it appeared as if she wanted to play innocent, but she seemed to change her mind. "I am well trained in how to keep it from contaminating me, and it comes in touch only with those I choose." She laughed. "Well, perhaps those pigs weren't intentional, but that wasn't entirely my fault. I stole one of the old sows who was about to die anyway to test the potency of my specimen. I didn't expect Lucas to find her and return her to the pens. That boy has been a problem, you know. I may have to harvest him early. He saw me bury the first heart, I'm sure. And when he dug it up, that's when the trouble started."

Alexandra stared at her, astonished. "But the men . . . How did you . . ."

"Men can be so vain! All I had to do when they came into the apothecary was suggest a bit of gel to soothe the roughness of their skin and then apply a little with a spatula. Even Harry fell for it."

"And when Ben Milligan didn't die of anthrax . . . What have you done with Nancy and the others?" Alexandra's fear was suddenly multiplied.

"Nancy?" Without taking her eyes off Alexandra, Polly took another step toward the two of them. Alexandra saw a bit of light signaling from the folds of Polly's skirt, and it was only then that she realized she was holding a scalpel. "There's no need to worry about poor little Nancy anymore," Polly continued. "You'll be joining her soon enough."

"Where is she?" Nicholas demanded.

Once again Polly stopped her slow, deliberate advance and turned her attention to him, her eyes now wild and blazing. "You're annoying me!" she said and at the same time slashed at him with the scalpel. Alexandra saw Nicholas raise his hands to fend off the attack and in almost the same instant saw his hands covered with blood. He backed away, and Polly slashed at him again. Nicholas cried out, bending at the waist, hitting his head on the table that held the microscope. He slumped to the floor as Polly kicked him.

Alexandra lunged toward him, but Polly was suddenly in front of her, close and looming. Instead of the slash Alexandra had expected, though, Polly lunged at her, not with her weapon, but with her body. In a sudden movement she pulled Alexandra's body close to hers and held the scalpel at her throat. Alexandra felt Polly's breath, hot and sweet, on her face as she spoke.

"I didn't want to have to do this, Dr. Gladstone. Neither to you nor to Nancy. In time I could have made you both understand, but you both got to be too suspicious, and I no longer had time."

Alexandra caught a glimpse of movement on the floor where Nicholas lay slumped, but she couldn't tell whether it was a sign of life or the throes of death that precipitated the movement. There was blood on his gloved hand and seeping from his midsection, staining his shirt. Polly was still talking, her lips moving very close to Alexandra's.

"You don't have families, you and Nancy, and I thought that would make you understand what I had to

do. You must know, don't you, that families are not supposed to be the way they are. We have to protect the
children from them, don't we? Like little Alice. She's a
sweet child, and we all love her. I love her. That's why
we must protect her. Her papa's not yet ripe for harvest-
ing, but he will be in time, won't he?"

When Alexandra didn't answer, Polly pushed the scalpel deeper into the skin of her neck, very near a scar
where an old wound had healed. "Don't ignore me!" Polly
shouted, spewing her spittle into Alexandra's mouth as
she spoke. "I'll carve your pretty neck with another scar
to match the one you already have. And ignoring me will
not stop me from doing what I have to do. You must
understand. It's what I must do because that's the only
way I can control them. I have to kill them to stop them
from hurting others the way he hurt me. The way he hurt
my mum. It made me sick the way she never tried to stop
him when he came at her, not even when he came at me.
It made me sick the way she gave up control."

"Polly, please," Alexandra whispered. "You must—"

"Don't tell me what I must do. I know! God has entered
me, and now I have become His flesh and His mind.
That's how I knew what I had to do when everyone
blamed that poor idiot and his mother. I'm sorry he found
the heart. I didn't mean for him to, and I did a poor job
on the second one's heart because I had to hurry, but I
couldn't let everyone go on thinking it was someone other
than God ridding the world of those men, those manufac-
turers of the devil's sperm. God is love. I am love, and
vengeance is mine. Love cannot thrive until the evil is
rooted out."

Alexandra felt the tip of the scalpel again, but in the
same moment, there was a tangle at her feet, and Polly
lost her balance. When she fell, her body toppled over a

crouched and bleeding Nicholas and landed facedown. The scalpel clattered to the floor only a few inches away from the arm she had thrust out to break her fall. In less than a second, Nicholas had straddled her and leaned forward to pin her arms, splayed over her head, to the floor.

He wasn't quick enough. She had already grasped the scalpel in her left hand, and in one surprisingly strong bucking motion, she forced Nicholas off her just enough to allow her to turn on her back. Facing him now, she swung the scalpel toward his chest in a stabbing motion, but he caught her wrist before the sharp tip hit its mark. It slashed the side of his face.

Alexandra watched the struggle, seeing the blood from Nicholas's hand and face stain the front of Polly's dress, her face, and arms. She quickly assessed that the wound on the side of his face was as superficial as her own neck wound, and judging from his quick movements, Nicholas's abdomen wound must be equally minor. It must have been the blow on his head when he fell that had rendered him temporarily unconscious.

But Polly still held the scalpel, and the danger wasn't over. Alexandra moved toward the two of them as they struggled on the floor. She felt helpless. What should she do?

It was then she heard a familiar sound and turned her attention toward the door that led out to the hallway of the inn. She heard it again. Closer.

A bark.

Zack's bark!

The door flew open, and Zack plunged into the room. He took only a fraction of a second to assess the circumstances then ran to Alexandra and tried to nudge her toward the door while he growled low in his throat. In the same moment, Rob and Artie rushed into the room behind

him, followed by Constable Snow. Both Rob and Snow
ran to Nicholas and Polly, but it was Rob who arrived
first. With a swift thrust of his foot, he kicked the scalpel
from Polly's hand. Snow then jerked her to her feet.

"You're under arrest, Miss Cobbe." He restrained her
with one of her arms twisted sharply behind her as he
held her facing away from him. She struggled very little.
Instead, she stared straight ahead at something invisible
to everyone else, her mouth opened slightly by a strange
small smile.

Alexandra cried out in a frightened voice. "Where is
Nancy?"

Polly turned to her with her burning eyes, still wearing
her secret smile, but she didn't speak. She only continued
to stare at her for what, to Alexandra, seemed a frightening and unnerving eternity.

"Zack can lead us to her," Artie cried.

Rob shook his head. "Zack doesn't understand how
to—"

"I was going to bury her. With the pigs. But I never
got around to finishing it." Polly's voice was oddly calm,
almost pleasant.

"Bury her?" Alexandra's voice trembled. "Is she—"

Polly suddenly jerked her body in a movement similar
to the one she used to turn herself over under Nicholas's
restraint. Snow lost his grip on her arm, and she might
have freed herself completely had not Nicholas moved
swiftly to force her arms to her sides, stopping her.

Alexandra saw the constable give a nod to Rob, and
for the first time she noticed the coiled rope Rob was
wearing, thrown over one shoulder and across his chest.
He removed the rope quickly, and before he could hand
it to Snow, Nicholas grabbed it and secured Polly's hands
behind her back.

Nicholas gave the knot one last pull. "There! You'll not escape from that."

Polly held her eyes on him as Snow led her across the room to the door. "Oh, I'll escape, sir," she said, still smiling. "And I'll be back. Mind you stay out of my way."

She let Snow lead her away, offering no resistance until he opened the door. With a sudden jerk, she turned and lunged at him, and before he could push her away or anyone could reach them, she sank her teeth into his lip. A fountain of blood spewed from where their mouths joined. Nicholas reached them first and forced Polly away from Snow while he kept a firm grip on her arms. She smiled at him, while the constable's blood dripped from the corners of her mouth.

Nicholas ignored her and turned to Snow. "Are you all right, Constable?"

Snow nodded while he dabbed his swelling lip, turning his once white handkerchief to the color of slaughter.

"I'll go with you," Nicholas said. He turned to Alexandra. "Stay here until I return, then I'll—"

Alexandra was already on her way to the door. "I'm going to find Nancy," she said, removing her gloves and tossing them aside.

"But where—"

"Seth Blackburn's pigs," she called over her shoulder as she hurried down the hall, Zack, Artie, and Rob following close behind.

"Did she mean Nancy's buried?" Artie asked, breathing hard from his efforts to keep up with the others.

"She's insane," Rob said. "We don't know what she meant."

Zack, caught up in the excitement of everyone racing through the streets of Newton-Upon-Sea, barked constantly as they ran and kept barking as they reached the edge of the village and ran the short distance into the rocky countryside where Seth's cottage and his pigpens stood.

Alexandra's lungs burned and her side ached, but she kept running until her feet were bogged in the muck surrounding the pens. The stench seared her nostrils and throat when she stopped, looking around wildly for some clue for where Nancy or her body could be. Rob was by her side offering a steadying hand when she stumbled. Zack kept up his barking and didn't stop even after Artie caught up. The three of them stood together, gasping for breath, their eyes anxiously searching the surroundings. The few pigs left, alarmed by Zack's noise, crowded together against the side of the pen and squealed with anger and annoyance, or perhaps with pain, as they pushed together tighter and tighter, trampling one another.

Seth's wife and two small boys stepped outside the cottage to investigate the racket. "What do you want!" Helen Blackburn asked, holding the baby and pulling Peter, the three-year-old, closer to her side. Her voice sounded frightened, and then, recognizing Alexandra, called out, "Dr. Gladstone? Is that you?"

"Helen!" Alexandra called. "We're looking for Nancy. Have you seen Nancy?"

Helen hurried toward Alexandra, still carrying the baby and holding Peter's hand. "You're looking for Nancy? Why do you think she's here?"

"Polly Cobbe told us she was—"

"Polly? The girl from the apothecary shop? Why would she think she was . . ." Helen stopped and glanced toward a small area of brush and trees. "I heard something earlier. Out there. I thought 'twas only the idjet boy, Lucas. He comes around sometimes. Likes to play with the pigs. Poor idjet. Don't know better."

"You heard something? What?" Alexandra asked. "What did you hear?"

"Well, 'twasn't Nancy, now was it? What would a nice girl like Nancy be doing out there?"

Alexandra turned toward the wooded area, hurrying away while Helen called after her. "Maybe 'twas just Lucas out there. Poor idjet. Don't know what 'e's doing 'alf the time."

Zack stayed close to Alexandra as she and the boys made their way into the outcropping. Behind them they heard Helen calling out to them. "They's nothing there save that old barn what's falling down. Be careful now, mind you."

Zack stopped suddenly, almost causing Alexandra to stumble over him. He barked, loud and excited, his ears turned back, his nose pointing to an area in front of them and slightly to the right.

Alexandra touched the top of his head. "What is it, Zack?"

"Is it Nancy?" Artie asked.

No one answered him, and Alexandra heard a sound, like the rustle of dry leaves. "Who's there?" she called.

There was only the sound of leaves again. Leaves being crushed. By someone's feet. Then something emerged from the shadows.

"Lucas? What are you doing here?" A mixture of emotions, annoyance, and relief flooded Alexandra's soul.

"I seen her," Lucas said, ignoring Alexandra's question. "I seen her hurt Nancy."

"Yes, Lucas. You saw Polly push Nancy, didn't you? Just as you told Rob. Go home now, Lucas. Your mother will be looking for you." Alexandra moved away from him, once again hurrying in the direction Helen had pointed.

"She was good to me and to me mum. She stopped them people from hurting mum, Polly did."

"Yes, Lucas, I know," Alexandra said, pushing branches away with abandon. Zack continued to bark, responding to her frantic movements.

"So why did she hurt Nancy?" Lucas asked, trying to keep up.

"I don't know, Lucas. Please go—" She slowed, breathing hard, when she saw the old stone barn. It was overgrown with vines on two sides, and half of the roof had collapsed. A heavy and weathered wooden door hung from one hinge, blocking the entrance.

"That's where I seen her," Lucas said. "I seen Polly carry something in there. I think 'twas Nancy."

Fear set afire the blood in Alexandra's veins, and she ran toward the barn. She didn't stop when she reached the door. Still running, she pushed the door with her outstretched hands, followed by her entire body. The door crashed to the earthen floor, sending up a cloud of dust. Zack, running beside her, barked even louder and continued to bark as the boys followed them inside the dark, shadowy space.

"Quiet, Zack!" Alexandra said. He didn't obey but continued to bark louder and louder as he stared into the corner at the same thing that held Alexandra's gaze. It was the form of a woman, half hidden by shadows, her skirts spread around her as she sat, leaning against the wall. Half of her face was missing.

"Oh God, 'tis Nancy!" Artie said, his words dissolving into sobs.

"Hush!" Rob commanded. "It ain't Nancy."

But it was. Alexandra recognized the dark muslin skirt. She took several slow steps toward her until she could hear her muffled sounds and see that it was a dirty rag tied around her mouth that, coupled with the shadows, had made it appear as if part of her face were missing. She dropped to her knees in the muck to untie the rag. Nancy's hair was matted and filthy and hung about her face in dirty ropes. Her dress was covered with grime and slime and held the same odor as the pigpens. Alexandra knew by the sound of Nancy's muffled voice and the fire that danced in her eyes that she was unhurt and that she would soon give them an earful.

Alexandra dropped the rag and stood to pull Nancy to her feet. Nancy spat the taste of pig filth from her mouth before the barrage started.

" 'Twas Polly that killed them. All of them. You have to hurry and tell the constable. Rob, you go, and take Artie with you. No, don't go! It may be dangerous. We must all leave. She's coming back for me. And she'll have you dead, too, Miss Alex. Said she'd kill us both because I finally saw 'twas she that killed . . . Said I was too clever for my own . . . Thank God you're . . . What took you so long? I've been here for days! Can you imagine? In this . . . I thought at least the boys would . . . Forgot you can't read. We must teach . . . What have the two of you been doing anyway? You're not hurt, are you? Polly didn't . . ."

"The constable has Polly. She's in gaol," Alexandra finally managed to say after several unsuccessful attempts to interrupt Nancy.

Nancy looked at Alexandra, her face, beneath the grime, now looking drawn and tired. A tear found its way down one cheek, plowing a pink row to her chin. Alexandra's own unshed tears made her eyes ache as she reached for Nancy to embrace her.

*   *   *

Alexandra had little time to talk with Nancy until morn-
ing. The night before, Nancy had washed her hair five
times and rinsed it with diluted vinegar, and she'd had
two soaking baths in steaming water, the last soak lasting
more than an hour. It was well past midnight when Alexandra heard her come upstairs to her room.

Yet Nancy was up early the next morning. She'd already fed the boys their breakfast and sent them out to
weed her herb garden when Alexandra came downstairs.
She had also prepared a breakfast of stewed tomatoes,
beef, and scones for the two of them.

Nancy took a sip of her tea and replaced the cup in its
saucer. " 'Twas Polly's apron that finally let me figure it
out," she said, in answer to the question Alexandra had
just asked.

"Her apron?"

"Yes. 'Twas Monday, you see, and I always do the
laundry on the second Monday of the month, you know.
Had that practice for years, I have. Just like my mum
before me."

"Yes, Nancy, I know," Alexandra said, trying not to
allow her impatience to show.

"Well, I was gathering the bed linens as I always do,
including the ones in the room where Polly was staying.
The one that used to be your father's, you know."

Alexandra nodded.

" 'Twas there I saw the apron. One of the big white
ones she always wears. Rather like the ones I wear, except
the stitching on mine is finer, and I always make certain
the cut is—"

"Nancy . . ."

"Impatient, aren't you?" Nancy said, taking a leisurely
sip of her tea. "And there's something else about you,
something that's . . . What happened to you in London?"

"For heaven's sake, Nancy, tell me about the apron!"

"Stained dark with blood."

"Polly brought a bloody apron here?"

Nancy nodded. "I found it in a drawer when I pulled it open for the clean sheets. 'Twas laying there on top of them. Polly walks in as I was standing there, holding it up a bit from the drawer. 'What are you doing?' she asks. 'Why, just changing the sheets,' I say. I felt uneasy, of course, as if I was meddling in her things. But I had made it clear to her that she could put her things in the other bureau, and I pointed out, just as you know I always do when there are guests, that the first bureau held the linens. If I didn't know better, I would think she wanted me to find that apron."

"Perhaps she did," Alexandra said, remembering what Dr. Mortimer had told her.

"You really think so?"

"Never mind. Please go on with your story."

"Oh yes, I was feeling guilty, as I said, but Polly finally just laughs it off and says she must have gotten the bureaus mixed in her mind. Said she meant to put it in the bottom drawer of her bureau where she put her soiled clothes. And as for the blood, she claimed 'twas her own. From her menses, she said. But anyone could see 'twasn't so. No woman bloodies the top of her apron with her monthlies, and even if she did, 'twould soak her dress first, and there was no sign of a soiled dress. She wore the same dress the whole time she was here."

Alexandra frowned and shook her head. "I don't understand how you would know immediately that she'd committed murder even if you knew it wasn't menstrual blood on her apron."

" 'Twasn't just that, of course. There were other things,

little things, before that, and the apron just put the cap on
it, as they say."

"What other things?"

Nancy shrugged. "It was strange things she did. When
I saw her tearing the pages from my novels of romance
and love. You know, the ones you dislike so much. I
never confronted her, but I found it odd that she would
tear out all references to any intimacy a man might have
with a woman. I didn't say anything, of course, because
I thought, since she is a Nonconformist, it might be some
kind of religious fanaticism. But then I saw her leave the
house at night, after she thought I was asleep, and she
wouldn't come back for hours. Once not until just before
dawn. And I found a scalpel in her room, before I found
the apron. 'Twas my cleaning day. You know I always
polish the furniture on the second Saturday of the month,
just as my mum did."

"Yes, yes, I know . . ."

"When I came into her room, there 'twas—a scalpel.
At first I thought 'twas one of yours. Thought she'd stolen
it, maybe. But when I looked closer, I knew 'twasn't
yours. It made me wonder, and I started thinking about
all the medical knowledge she has. She just might have
surgical skills, I thought. But 'twasn't 'til that apron that
I put it all together and began to think it could be a woman
who killed those men. It could be Polly. I wasn't really
certain, though, until she confronted me. Said she knew I
had guessed the truth. Said I'd have to die. Now that gave
me a fright if I ever had one! She made me leave at knife
point, but when I left, I didn't lock the house, and I left
Zack here, thinking the boys would think something was
wrong and come looking for me. Even if they couldn't
read the note I left." She gave a little derisive laugh.

"They did look for you," Alexandra said. "They just

couldn't find you. And we're all lucky she didn't kill you."

"I don't think she wanted to. Not really," Nancy said. "That's another thing strange about her. I couldn't help getting the feeling she didn't have the courage to kill me. Yet she seemed to have no trouble at all killing the others."

"They were all men, Nancy. And you're a woman. That's why she couldn't kill you. Remember, you're the one who pointed out that fact to me."

"I did, that's true," Nancy said. "But why did she choose only men?"

"When I saw Dr. Mortimer in London . . ."

"What happened to you in London?"

Alexandra ignored her. "Dr. Mortimer said—" A knock on the surgery door interrupted her before she could begin to explain the alienist's theories to Nancy. It was Evelyn Murray, who had walked from the village to ask the doctor to come have a look at her eight-year-old son, who had a terrible cough. Alexandra left immediately to care for the boy who, she soon learned, had whooping cough, evidence that the disease had not yet run its course in Newton-Upon-Sea. She used the rest of the morning to complete her usual rounds to visit patients at home, making Tom and Kate Hastings's home her last stop.

When she arrived home around noon, she was surprised to see Nicholas Forsythe in the parlor, engaged in a casual conversation with Nancy. The thought that Nancy might have been prodding him to learn whether anything had happened between the two of them filled her with dread. They both greeted her with guilty smiles, which made her even more suspicious.

Nicholas rose to his feet. "Good afternoon, Dr. Gladstone."

"Good afternoon, Mr. Forsythe," she said and glanced at Nancy, who was also now standing, pretending to be busy.

"I must say, I'm rather surprised to see you here," Alexandra said, turning back to Nicholas. "I should have thought the Montmarsh case would have taken you back to London immediately."

"It seems I've had something of a reprieve from that case."

"Really?" Alexandra said, removing her gloves and placing them on top of the medical bag she'd set on the hall table. "Let's have a look at those wounds."

"What? Oh no, they're quite all right," he said with a wave of his hand. "Nancy's given them all the attention they need."

"So the Montmarsh case has been settled? There's a new heir?"

"I just received a telegram a few hours ago informing me of that."

"A telegram? Of course? How did we ever live without them?" There was a weary sound to her voice. She continued to eye Nancy suspiciously.

Nancy responded by making herself busy gathering up the tea dishes she'd used to serve Nicholas. "And how are our patients?" she asked, just as Alexandra was about to ask Nicholas who had inherited Montmarsh and been named the sixth earl of Dunsford.

"Most are doing quite well," she said in answer to Nancy's question. "The Murray boy has whooping cough, but I expect him to recover nicely."

"Very good. And the Hastings baby?" Nancy was working terribly hard at playing innocent.

"Alice's cough has improved, and her breathing's less

labored. As you said, her cough will linger for weeks, perhaps even months."

Nancy turned to her, a worried look on her face.

"It's too early to know if the disease has damaged her brain," Alexandra said, reading the question in Nancy's eyes.

Nancy shook her head. "It so often does in infants."

"A disease of the brain?" Nicholas asked.

"The disease is whooping cough," Alexandra said. "The hard cough can cause damage to a young child's brain. We can only pray Alice will be spared that fate along with the superstition and ridicule and misunderstanding that accompany it."

"A brain injury?" Nicholas said, musing. "Is it possible all insanity is nothing more than physical disorder as the old-fashioned phrenologists claim?"

"That debate rages still," Alexandra said. "Are insanity and monomania and hysteria and imbecility and idiocy, mechanical failures? Or is there some other reason, as Dr. Mortimer's radical views suggest? Would you care to join us for lunch, Mr. Forsythe? I must eat hurriedly in order to open my surgery on time."

"Your invitation is very kind, but I . . . Of course," he said, seeming to reconsider on the spur of the moment. "I'd be happy to stay. So kind of you to ask."

"Our luncheon is customarily informal, Mr. Forsythe. In the kitchen."

"I should be delighted to—"

" 'Tis no longer Mr. Forsythe, miss, 'tis Lord Dunsford," Nancy said, interrupting.

Alexandra found she couldn't speak. She could only stare in shock, first at Nancy and then at Nicholas.

Nicholas gave her a shy smile. "I hope you will never burden me by addressing me with that title."

"You . . ."

"I'm as surprised as you are," Nicholas said. "It's a complicated story, of course, but you knew, didn't you, that I was related to the late Lord Dunsford on my mother's side? My older brother, of course, had claim to the title by right of progeny, but he refused it. I know, it's hard to believe, unless you know my brother. But he has already inherited a title from my mother's side of the family, along with a considerable amount of land, and he will, of course, inherit from our father, so it was his wish that I—"

"Lord Dunsford?" Alexandra said, interrupting him. She was still in shock. "Forgive me for suggesting that we eat in the—"

"Must I remind you that I've dined in your kitchen in the past and found it quite enjoyable?"

Alexandra was still stunned. "Of course," she said when she could regain her voice. She gave him a cordial smile and led the way. Nicholas sat in a chair across from her, the wide and badly scarred table surface separating them while they waited for Nancy to set their meal in front of them.

"You may be interested to know, I had a chat with the veterinarian from Colchester who came here to examine Blackburn's swine," Nicholas said. He seemed eager to get away from the subject of his newly acquired title.

"Indeed?" Alexandra, nevertheless, still felt a bit uncomfortable with the idea of his being elevated to the peerage.

"Yes, he confirmed anthrax, but he seems to think it will not be too difficult to control. It seems swine are more resistant to the germ than other animals."

"How fortunate," Alexandra said. "Polly has certainly wrought enough trouble for Newton as it is."

"Yes, but I still find it frustrating that we shall never know for certain whether her insanity was caused by a mechanical failure in her brain or by something else," Nicholas said.

"It is frustrating, yes," Alexandra said, doing her best to regain her mental equilibrium. "We can only know that she is insane, whatever the cause."

"She won't hang, will she? Poor girl," Nancy said.

Nicholas didn't notice the inappropriateness of her inserting herself in the conversation. He'd obviously gotten to know Nancy well enough during his previous visits to be neither surprised nor shocked at her behavior. "Polly won't hang," he said. "The law will protect her because she's insane. She'll live the rest of her life in an asylum."

"Will she?" Alexandra asked. She felt a chill as she remembered Polly's last words to Constable Snow before she was taken away.

I'll be back. Mind you stay out of my way.

Author's Note

The portions of the dialogue attributed to Florence Nightingale are, for the most part, taken from her letters and papers as researched by Hugh Small and included in his book, *Florence Nightingale: Avenging Angel*, St. Martin's Press, 1998.